IN
PURSUIT
OF A
NEW
DAWN

Anirban 'Andy' Bhattacharyya studied engineering at the Birla Institute of Technology and Science, India, and did his MBA from the Fuqua School of Business at Duke University. He founded Amplo Global Inc. in 2019, an artificial intelligence-led sustainability risk analysis organization, which has transformed the way an organization executes risk management and carbon accounting through data strategy.

Andy is a sustainability leader, climate risk advisor, *Forbes Magazine* author, patent holder, TEDx speaker and an adviser to technology startups. He is also the author of a novel, *The Ruins of Hope*, and a business book, *Industry 5.0 and Data Economy: Precursor to Embracing ESG and AI Led Transformation*.

Find more about him at:
https://www.facebook.com/Anirbanauthoraswell/
https://www.instagram.com/andy_authoraswell/
https://twitter.com/AndyInnovation

IN
PURSUIT
OF A
NEW
DAWN

A COLLECTION OF
SHORT STORIES

ANIRBAN BHATTACHARYYA

RUPA

Published by
Rupa Publications India Pvt. Ltd 2024
7/16, Ansari Road, Daryaganj
New Delhi 110002

Sales Centres:
Bengaluru Chennai
Hyderabad Jaipur Kathmandu
Kolkata Mumbai Prayagraj

P-ISBN: 978-93-6156-472-7
E-ISBN: 978-93-6156-458-1

First impression 2024

10 9 8 7 6 5 4 3 2 1

The moral right of the author has been asserted.

Printed in India

Contents

1

The Funeral

It is two days after Holi—the vibrant festival of colour and mirth. The usually quiet lane in the leafy neighbourhood of Lokhandwala has changed, now filled with a fleet of cars, gleaming in the spring sunshine and lining the street. Parking in these parts is typically difficult on a regular day, but today has been a chaotic ordeal. At Shanti Bhavan, the two-storey whitewashed bungalow located on the corner block of the neighbourhood, there is a bustle of activity, reminiscent of a flutter of butterflies in spring. On the cool porch, sandals and shoes are littered on the steps. To the left of the main door, there is a large framed photograph of a young man. He has dark curly hair, a thin face with a strong jawline, sparkling eyes and a smile that reaches his eyes. The photograph is carefully garlanded with strings of yellow marigolds.

Inside, the living room has been cleared out. The sofas have been pushed to the corners, and chairs, rented from a nearby funeral service, are laid out neatly against the walls. A makeshift stage has been placed at one end of the room. It is not high, just a few inches off the floor. There are around twenty-five people in the room—friends and family—dressed in white and wearing sombre expressions. The news of Manan's death came so suddenly that many close relatives are still on flights, buses and trains, making their way here. They even missed the actual funeral service, which was held the previous day.

Mrs Pooja Chatterjee's eyes are red and swollen as she converses with a middle-aged relative, who attempts to console her. Little do they know that nothing they say will ever make this pain go away. *If only they knew what she knew.* Instead, she asks if everyone has been served tea. Tea always helps, no matter the enormity of the calamity. Sometimes another thought crosses her mind. If this hadn't happened, she would've been on the set of the latest Bengali blockbuster, wrapping up a film that had been three years in the making. She had dedicated every second of these years to this film and the thought stabbed at her heart with a pain she did not know how to manage.

Across the room, Pooja's ex-husband, Girish Chatterjee, is inconsolable. In complete contrast to his ex-wife, Girish let out a wail; his loud sobs piercing the hearts of some of the guests, while making a few others cringe in embarrassment. This is a side of Girish that no one who knows him has encountered before. Usually, he is a calm, reserved person who rarely speaks unless required. He is never ruffled and never at a loss. Yet today, he is broken.

Anandita, Girish's niece, approaches Pooja. 'Mami,' she begins, 'it's three o'clock, shall we begin with the speeches?'

Pooja, who has been wrapped up in thought, looks up at Anandita, and for a moment doesn't recognise the young girl who seems to be asking her something.

'Shall we begin the speeches, Mami?' Anandita asks again, tenderly.

'The speeches...yes...yes. We'd better get started. Don't want to keep people waiting for too long,' Pooja replies. 'Why don't you ask Girish Mama if he'd like to start?'

'Okay, Mami,' Anandita murmurs, and she makes her way across the room to Girish. She speaks to him in a low whisper. Girish wipes his eyes even though the tears don't seem to stop and shakes his head as if to compose himself.

'Yes, beta,' Girish says, as he stands up. 'I'll start.'

He walks to the stage. His shoulders are hunched, his hair dishevelled and his white kurta is in a crumpled state.

'Hello,' he begins with a croak. But no one seems to notice, so the guests continue talking amongst themselves.

Anandita approaches Girish and addresses the crowd. 'Hi everyone, can I please have your attention?'

A few folks turn to look at her.

'Can everyone please settle down? We are going to begin the speeches with Girish Mama,' she pleads, squeezing Girish's hand before walking away.

The hall falls silent as Girish clears his throat. He adjusts his glasses and smoothens his kurta. When he opens his mouth to speak, the words are soft and shaky.

'Hello everyone,' he sputters. 'Firstly, I'd like to thank all of you for coming here today. It means a lot to me and...,' he hesitates for a second '...Pooja, that you took the time to be with us at such a tragic moment in our lives.' He takes out a handkerchief from his pocket and blows his nose.

'Let me tell you this right at the outset. I have never been good at speeches and things like that. I don't know if what I'm going to say is going to make sense to anyone here because I am not the most eloquent in the family. If my son, Manan, were here today, he'd know exactly what to say, because he had a certain way with words. He was a writer; did you know that? Well, he hadn't been published but that was his dream. In fact, one of the first memories I have of Manan is of him writing a short story. I mean, of course, I remember things about him before this memory, but this is the one that came to my mind this morning.

'Manan was perhaps six years old at the time. He had been working on a short story all weekend. And it was a Sunday evening when he came to us, proudly announcing that he had finally completed it and wanted to read it out to us.' Girish stops to smile. 'The story was about a family...a happy family...who encountered great adversity. The father had lost his job and the mother had fallen ill. Their son was deeply saddened by the family's distress. So the child goes about making his parents feel better. He does odd chores for his neighbour and earns some money. He also prepares soup for his mother to help her feel better. In the end, the father secures employment and the mother recovers. The family comes out of this situation intact, as if nothing had ever happened; as if they'd never suffered.' Girish pauses for a breath. 'There is no doubt that the story was about our family. My son was always perceptive regarding our faults and challenges, and he tried his best to make us all feel better.' Girish lowers his eyes, his voice trailing off. 'Even though things cannot always be fixed.'

'My son was better than me. He was hopeful. He was a sensitive, compassionate man who always put others before him. He was more like a parent to...us...' Girish looks in Pooja's direction '...than we were to him, and I deeply regret that. I remember him being curious about everything the world had to offer. He loved books, art and music. Often I'd drop him off at events—debates, speeches and various school events. He would always be so excited about the different competitions at school and would register himself for all of them if he was eligible.' Girish takes another pause as he reminisces. 'If only...if only we had been better parents to him, then perhaps a father wouldn't have to speak about his son like this.'

It is evident that Girish cannot continue any longer. His face is contorted and tears stream down his cheeks. He hangs his head and his glasses slip to the bridge of his nose. An elderly gentleman holds him by the shoulder and guides him to his chair.

The sound of another chair scraping against the floor can be heard as Pooja rises. She is around sixty but appears younger than her age. Her skin is firm, and her posture is poised and erect. The only sign of distress is the few strands of hair that have escaped her otherwise impeccable bun. As she makes her way to the stage, she glances at her ex-husband and a look of remorse shoots across her face. Nonetheless, she tightly wraps the *pallu* of her white sari around her head before stepping on to the makeshift stage. She begins talking, even though Girish's sobs can still be heard in the hall.

'Thank you for that, Girish...and thank you everyone for coming to support our family at a time like this. I don't know what we would do without you. I don't know why I decided to do this...this speech-giving thing, because I am in no state to talk about...my son. He was just the most won—,' her voice breaks, 'wonderful son and human being, and it pains me no end that he had to go before I did. Which mother can bear a catastrophe like this?'

The guests listen in rapt attention to Pooja's words.

'Those of you who know me know that I cannot keep secrets from my family, so what I'm going to say now is going to come as a shock to all of you,' Pooja blurts. As she tucks away the errant strands of her hair behind her ear, she continues, 'The truth is that I knew this day would come; it was just a matter of time.' Her statement is followed by pin-drop silence. Girish looks up at his wife, confusion clearly evident on his face. 'Call it a mother's instinct or plain old intuition, but somehow I knew that this fate would befall Manan.'

An elderly woman at the back gasps. The other guests look at each other in horror and confusion.

'What are you talking about, Pooja?' Girish croaks.

'Of course you are shocked by this, but the truth is sad—it was going to happen. You see, Girish only saw his son through rose-tinted glasses. He couldn't see that his son was struggling. Perhaps he couldn't bear to think of it because the thought itself pained him greatly. But as a mother I saw the signs. He was listless and unfocused. I regret not speaking to him about what was going on in his mind. I secretly hoped that he would get better and I didn't know whether he would have liked me talking to him even. Do you understand how that makes me feel? Or how I'll spend the rest of my days burdened by this guilt? My son's death was no accident; neither was it a natural one. My son committed suicide,' she shouts, bursting into tears.

'Pooja!' Girish admonishes, gaping at her.

The guests gasp audibly, and as the news spreads across the hall, questions are asked, and voices rise until Pooja's voice is barely audible.

'...please, I know,' Pooja continues talking despite the crescendo, 'but it is the truth, and all of you—our friends and family—should know the truth. On the morning of Holi, my son consumed a lot of drugs. He overdosed and died.'

Pooja begins to ramble, 'We should never have let him go to the US... It was all your idea, Girish. It was you who encouraged him to leave his home...when I told him to study here! Who knows how lonely he felt, whether he was suffering from depression there... But no one listens to me in this family...'

'This is madness! Stop it!' Girish pleads, as he lowers his head into his hands, fresh tears welling up in his eyes. The gentleman sitting beside him holds him by his shaking shoulders, trying to calm him down.

'Why are you saying all this?' a relative bursts out. 'Isn't it enough that your son has passed away?'

Pooja wipes her eyes. She is silent for a while, then she says, 'Usko jaana hi tha.' (He had to go.)

A middle-aged lady in a white sari approaches Pooja and takes her hand. 'Come, *bou*, come, sit down,' she says, coaxing Pooja like a child.

Pooja steps down from the stage, goes to the farthest corner of the room and takes a seat.

For a moment, everyone refrains from making any sudden movements. Conversations become muted, taking place in small groups with hushed tones. Then a thin and tall 50-year-old man gets up from his chair and makes his way to the stage in slow, measured strides. He stands on the stage and looks around the room, the creases on his forehead deepening.

'For those of you who don't know me, my name is Sudhir and I have been the Chatterjees' neighbour for the last 25 years.'

The guests fall silent as they turn to listen to Sudhir.

'This unfortunate event has disturbed me greatly. Manan was too young to depart from life now. He had an entire lifetime ahead of him, waiting to be lived... The thing is, I've known Manan since he was a child. I've seen him grow up, play, make friends, go off to America and get a great job. I've seen him just as I've seen myself age.' He stops speaking to dab his forehead with a handkerchief. 'It is not my place to say these things, but I don't believe he killed himself.' He waits for the news to sink in.

The silence in the room is so thick that you can almost slice it with a knife.

'Manan was a magnanimous guy with a big heart. It is very hard to find young people like him these days. Ever since Manan came back from the US, and actually even before that, he was always available to help us old folks with our errands. He would spend many days in my hot basement, fixing things, and would fetch groceries for me when I was ill. He used to check up on me every weekend to see if I needed anything. He didn't need to, but he did. Manan genuinely cared for his community and people. He had a large heart and a generous disposition. How can a person who has so much love to give want to kill himself?'

Pooja bursts into tears.

'I am sorry, Girish,' Sudhir says. 'I think Pooja has got this wrong and it's very distressing to think about it. I just want to tell you what a lovely son you and Pooja had raised and we, especially me, are very grateful and lucky to have had him in our lives. I am very sorry for your loss.'

'Well, I think you've said enough, Sudhir,' Pooja snaps.

Sudhir senses Pooja's hostility, sighs, and then exits the stage. Just then, Mrs Rewaz, the Chatterjees' other neighbour, a 75-year-old woman, stands up with the help of her walking stick. She takes a while to reach the stage and no one notices her doing so. She doesn't get up on the stage; instead, she hits her walking stick on its side—two loud knocks—to get everyone's attention.

Mrs Rewaz speaks slowly, with a stammer. 'I don't know what you guys are going on about. We are at a funeral, for God's sake. The least you can do is show some respect. To Pooja and Girish, I can only give you my deepest condolences. I am truly sorry for your loss. No parent deserves such a tragedy,' she coughs.

'The only reason I've come here today is for Manan, who was a lovely child, God bless his soul. He helped me with my plumbing and groceries and even drove me to my daughter's house a few times. I agree with Sudhir, I can't believe such a fine young man would…' she trails off, glaring at Pooja. 'Sudhir is right. We have seen Manan grow from a lovely child into a wonderful man. It is rare to find young people who would help the elderly, let alone even notice we are around.' She pauses.

'I have seen him help all sorts of people. In fact, every afternoon, as I'd sit by the front window having my cup of tea, I would see a young man come by the Chatterjees' house. Manan would graciously open the door for him and let him in. The young man would stay for a few hours and leave at 5 p.m. I thought about this a lot. The young man obviously needed some kind of help, and how kind Manan was not to turn him down—day after day, even though he probably had his own work and responsibilities to take care of. Pooja and Girish must be in shock because I can't imagine how it must feel to lose your only son. I wish you both strength and may God bless you.' Saying this, Mrs Rewaz hobbles back to her chair with the help of a young girl.

No one notices, but Pooja's face has turned to stone. She mutters to no one, 'You saw him too?'

An image flashes in her mind's eye.

It is the morning of Holi and Pooja has taken the day off from her shoot to be with her son. She is contemplating making biryani and phirni for lunch. She can't recall the last time she spent Holi or any other festival with him. Her career took over after her divorce and she wouldn't have it any other way. Being a woman in a man's world is challenging, but even more so when one is divorced and has to stand on her own feet to provide for herself.

She goes to the kitchen and starts taking out the ingredients she had bought the previous evening—onions, mutton, rice, garlic and potatoes. She is going to make her famous mutton biryani—a recipe passed down her family over generations. Manan is in his room upstairs, finishing up some work on his laptop.

Pooja hums as she meticulously arranges the ingredients on the kitchen counter, then begins to wash, chop and grate. Just like at work, she is consumed by the process and doesn't realize how time flies by.

Hours later, the kitchen and living room are filled with the aroma of cooking. As she assembles the mutton with the rice, she hears the doorbell. Leaving the kitchen, she hurries to the door, mindful not to leave the cooker unattended for long, lest the rice burn.

As she opens the door, a harsh beam of sunlight bursts into the cool living room. A well-built man in his mid-twenties is standing on the porch, a bunch of flowers in his hands. He is smiling, but as soon as he sees Pooja, his smile disappears and he becomes motionless.

'Yes?' Pooja asks him. 'What do you want?'

'I-I...' the young man stammers.

'Go on...' she says impatiently.

Just then, they hear the sound of footsteps coming down the stairs, which seem to stop on the last step.

'Ma...' Manan says, his voice heavy with emotion.

'What is it?' Pooja asks, looking from her son to the young man on the porch.

'I...' Manan hesitates.

Pooja turns to the young man. 'Who are you looking for?'

The young man looks at Manan and then Pooja. Finally, he replies, 'I'm here for Manan, aunty.'

'Manan?' Pooja looks confused.

'Ma...I can explain...' Manan says, his voice weighed down by emotion.

Then, something shifts in the atmosphere. Pooja looks at the young man—his heavy lashes, *kohl*-rimmed eyes, the way his trousers hang around his hips...and she looks at her son—his face flushed, his breathing heavy and a certain gleam in his eye. She understands.

For a moment, no one moves. They are frozen in time. Then, Pooja snaps back to reality.

'Get out of my house,' she says through gritted teeth. 'Now!' and she slams the door.

'Ma!' Manan croaks.

'What...what is going on, Manan?' Pooja turns around to face her son, a vein pulsing in her forehead. 'Who was that? Tell me now!'

'Ma... Ma...' Manan stammers. 'He's my...friend.' The last word is a mere whisper.

'Friend?' Pooja shouts, looking like she is about to explode. 'Tell me the truth... Is he just a friend or someone more?'

Manan doesn't speak. Instead, tears roll down his face.

'Talk to me, son...' Pooja says, her words laden with bitterness.

'Ma...' Manan says through his tears. 'He's more than a friend.'

'I knew it!' Pooja snaps. 'You're...you're...a homo—'

Manan breaks down. 'I'm sorry, Ma... I'm really sorry. That is who I am. I can't change it...'

Pooja gasps. Her face is contorted with a mixture of confusion, anger and desperation. 'After all we've done for you. Loved you, sent you to a fancy school in the US...this is what you give us! What will people say? That my son is a homosex—' She can't bring herself to say the word.

Manan falls to his knees and sobs like a broken man on the step.

The room is filled with his cries and Pooja's voice. 'God! What will we do? What did I do wrong?'

Then, Manan gets up, wipes his tears and speaks in a low and quivering voice. 'Don't worry, Ma. I'll fix it.'

But Pooja barely hears the words; her blood is pounding in her ears. She sits down on the sofa and cries. She doesn't notice that Manan has turned around and is climbing up the stairs.

It is a while before Pooja musters the strength to get up. The rice on the stove has burnt, filling the downstairs room with its strong smell.

She rushes to the kitchen to save what she can, but it is too late. The dish is ruined beyond repair.

⌀

Pooja tries to shake off the memory, but it bears down on her. She begins to wail like a wounded animal.

The guests around her look surprised. A few try to console her, but she pushes them away and tears at her hair.

'What have I done? What have I done? Oh, my son... my son!' she repeats the words over and over again.

Girish walks over to her and holds her in his arms. 'It's okay, Pooja... it's okay, Pooja... hush hush.'

'He went upstairs and never came down...' She sobs into his chest. 'He never came down.'

'I know, Pooja,' Girish says softly. 'I know.'

2

Daughter of the Night

The vast sky spread across the land like an unending slate, interrupted only by the serrated tops of the densely forested hills looming over the landscape. The brilliant light, casting the hills in green, was quickly fading, turning a pale yellow as it angled over the hills, gently disappearing over their edges. Spikes of thin light impaled the treeline and the air grew cooler. As the sun finally dipped behind the hills and the light faded, the sky turned dark like a pitch-black cloak, with millions of stars embroidered in its fabric. The trees became dark and grey, resembling an army ready for battle.

These were the hills of refuge, where one could go and lose themselves forever. In the tropical jungle, rich with vegetation and animal life, the pawprints of a panther sometimes appeared next to the footprints of a farmer. Here, ferns and forest lace intertwined with giant colocasia, vying for space, while the forest floor was abundant with critters and nourishing red loamy soil.

Amidst the darkness of the forest, a few lights sparkled. Were it not for the kerosene lamps illuminating a small mud hut nestled at the foothills, one might never know that people lived in these parts.

The mud hut belonged to a farmer, Ajay, and his daughter, Pooja. Ajay had received this parcel of land as dowry when he married. When his wife died during childbirth, leaving him with an infant daughter to care for, he decided that the family needed a larger space than their cramped home in Siliguri Town. With just two other contractors, Ajay embarked on the task of building a home for his daughter and himself. As a farmer, he had limited funds at his disposal, so he constructed their home from whatever the forest offered: pine from the surrounding trees, mud from the riverbanks and thatch from dried bamboo. It took him six months to complete it, after which he paid the local pandit to bless their home before bringing his daughter and mother to live at the edge of the forest, in the lap of nature.

All of this transpired many years ago. Ajay, now 75 years old, observed his daughter, Pooja, who had blossomed into a dark-skinned beauty with shimmering eyes; thick, long, glossy hair tied into a fat braid; and shapely calves honed from the daily labour of hill life.

Since she had grown up in nature, forgoing school and a formal education because of the costs involved, Pooja knew these lands and hills like the back of her hand. She was soft-footed and quiet, acquainted with every birdcall and tree. She anticipated the rains and the forest's offerings of special fruits, hidden from the hungry eyes of the townsfolk. Pooja helped her father in the farmlands when she wasn't milking the cows, cooking, fetching water or cleaning the house. She was a good daughter, Ajay thought, unlike the young women in town with their painted faces and loud *saris*. Pooja spoke only when she was asked a question and was never rude. She sang melodious folk songs about the moon and rain while cooking, which soothed the old man's soul, lulling him to sleep.

When Pooja turned twenty-five, her father expanded their home to include another room to provide her with some privacy. He often broached the subject of marriage during their meals on the cool mud floor, remarking, 'Girls your age already have children. I will not be around forever to look after you. You need to start a family of your own.' Pooja's response would be a mumbled, 'I am not ready, Father.'

Although Ajay received numerous proposals for his daughter, he was hesitant to impose them upon her. After his mother's passing, Pooja was all he had. Even though his peers mocked him, labelling him a sentimental old fool for allowing his daughter to grow old without a man, he didn't have the heart to send her away to a stranger and his home.

Ajay made a trip to town once every two weeks, where he procured odds and ends for the home: hinges, rope and sometimes a bar of soap, a luxury he delighted in bringing for his daughter. After he was done pottering about the marketplace, he'd often visit a small, battered tea shop where three or four of his friends frequently gathered. They would order cups of tea and some fried yams, discussing their days.

During one of these visits, as Ajay settled down in the tea shop with his friends, he sensed an unusual tension in their demeanour. They seemed distant and reluctant to engage with him.

'Is something the matter?' Ajay enquired, reaching for the cup of tea brought by a young boy clad in a dhoti, balancing a large tray of their beverages and snacks. 'You are turning up your noses at me as though I have stepped on some cow dung on the way and brought its stench with me.'

The men didn't laugh, shifting awkwardly on the hard, wobbly bench, avoiding his gaze. Bablu, Ajay's childhood friend, wearing glasses and a faded blue shirt tucked into his dhoti, finally spoke up.

'My friend, how to tell you this...'

The others looked away.

'Tell me what?' asked Ajay.

Bablu took a moment before speaking. 'The thing we want to tell you is not easy. But tell you we must. You see, how long have I known you, *bondhu*?'

'Since we were wee tots...' Ajay replied, curiosity in his eyes. 'You know you can tell me anything.'

'That's just it,' said Bablu. 'This is not anything. This is very serious.'

'Then cough it up,' Ajay said firmly, the mirth vanishing from his eyes.

Silence fell upon the group once again.

'Oh, this is difficult. I never thought I would see the day when I had to utter such words...' said Bablu.

'Why don't you cut to the chase then...' said Ajay.

'Your daughter is a prostitute,' Bablu spat out the words.

For a minute, stunned silence enveloped the tea stall. Then, Ajay felt his hands shake. 'Wha—' he uttered.

Bablu looked down at his tea cup.

'What?' Ajay tried again, the words knotted in his throat. 'How dare you say something like that! Especially you, my friend.'

Bablu looked his friend squarely in the eye. 'It breaks my heart to tell you this because you are my friend and I know how much that girl means to you. I have seen you raise her from a wailing infant to the woman she has grown into. I have seen you sacrifice everything for her and yet...' Bablu paused. 'Here we are,' he said, turning his palms upwards on the table as if to indicate that this was the working of fate and nothing they could do would have stopped the course of events.

'What do you mean, "here we are"?' Ajay's voice trembled. He could feel the anger rise within him, bubbling up through his stomach, filling his chest and burning a path up his throat to the point he couldn't breathe.

'Everyone in town is talking about it,' Mohan whispered.

'Everyone who?' said Ajay. 'Talking about what?'

Bablu took a deep breath. 'The rumour going around town is that every night, after midnight, people have seen a man going into Pooja's room—the quarter you had built for her some years ago—the extension. Some folks have said that these are all different men. They come in at night and leave before dawn. This can only mean one thing…'

Ajay opened his mouth to speak, but no words came out.

'Have you not heard or seen anything?' said Mohan.

'No, I have not…' managed Ajay. 'Pooja would never…'

'But it is the talk of the town,' said Mohan. 'Surely you must have heard *something*?'

Mohan's insistence triggered something within Ajay and he snapped. He stood up abruptly, pushing against the table, spilling three cups of tea at once. 'NO!' he yelled. 'I haven't heard or seen anything! You are mongrels, all of you, to cast my daughter in such a light. Shame on you, all of you.'

With that outburst, Ajay stormed out of the tea stall, through the marketplace, and up into the cool, winding hills until he reached his home.

'The truth is always hard to swallow,' Mohan said to the rest once Ajay had left. 'But it is good we told him. He needs to know what his daughter has been up to. Shame, what a lovely girl she was, and yet this is what happens when daughters are not married off at the right age. Like fruit, they ripen and then they turn bad.'

Ajay was engulfed in a dark mood. All the way home, the words swirled through his mind. His Pooja? His daughter? No, it couldn't be. Something was wrong. Not his daughter. The one who sang songs of the moon and rain, the one who called out to birds and herded the sheep and milked the cows like Radha. His daughter who patiently cooked him hot chapatis, one after another, only ate once her father was done. The one who woke up before him and prayed to Durga Ma every morning after bathing and before doing anything else. Impossible!

Yet, like a seed planted into fertile soil, the idea took hold, growing tiny fibrous roots in his mind. Why was his daughter so quiet, so content in leading this solitary life in the forest with her father? Why did she not crave a married life, a family and children of her own? Why didn't she want to go into town and buy *bindis* and face powder, or socialize with women her own age?

Something was not right and the mere thought of it broke his poor old heart.

That night, Ajay watched his daughter with new eyes as she served him a fluffy hot roti. He scrutinized her like a hawk, yet there was nothing in his daughter's expression or demeanour to suggest anything out of the ordinary. No, his daughter was not a prostitute. She was still his untarnished angel.

And yet…

Why was she so composed? So sure? Her hands so steady? Her gaze so calm and unruffled? Where was the lifeblood of a young woman?

After finishing dinner, Ajay made a show of going to bed. He told Pooja that he was feeling tired and would go straight to sleep, forgoing smoking his pipe. It was a ritual—every night after dinner, Ajay smoked a pipe to keep his daughter company as she ate, and while she washed the dishes and tidied the kitchen.

In the charpoy in his room, he listened to the sounds of her chewing, the thin gold bangles on her wrists clinking as she washed the dishes and mopped the floor. Then, he heard the sound of the door being bolted and the windows being shuttered. A louder creak indicated that she had opened the door that connected the main hut to her extension.

Then, silence.

Ajay waited with the patience of a ravenous tiger, yet he was also as alert as its prey. He listened to the creatures of the forest—the crickets chirping outside, the frogs croaking in their ponds—and the rustle of the trees as the wind swept through the forest foliage.

He waited and waited, hoping that there would be nothing

so that he could go into town and confront Mohan and Bablu, and call them liars for attempting to ruin his daughter's pristine reputation. He thought about the choicest abuses he would hurl at them, crafting the right sentence that would strike where it would hurt them most. Hours passed like this. As he lay on his charpoy, contemplating these scenarios, he thought he heard something. The sound was different. It was not a sound of the forest. It was faint and Ajay had to strain his ears to hear it, but there was no mistaking it.

It was the steady, muffled sound of footsteps against fallen leaves.

Ajay froze.

In the distance, Ajay thought he heard the faint creak of a door opening. It was so faint he would have never heard it if he had been asleep, but now with his senses on alert, he did. He sat up in his bed, sweat prickling his grey-haired scalp. His heart throbbed loudly in his chest, as if the entire forest could hear it. He rose, steadying himself by holding on to the edge of the charpoy. The only light in the room was from the moonlight streaming in through the open window. He softly walked out of his room and into the hall, which doubled up as their eating and cooking area. At the main door, he paused to collect himself. Slowly and carefully, he unlatched the bolt and stepped outside into the night.

Ajay padded down the steps of his hut, feeling the damp

earth against his soles. He kept to the side, staying in the shadows as he crept along towards the extension where his daughter slept.

Unlike his throbbing heart, the night was deathly still. He was only a few feet from his daughter's window now, and yet it seemed like there was no one there. He hoped against hope that his friends had been wrong.

As he reached Pooja's window, he crouched as much as his old knees would allow him. He took a moment to brace himself. What would he see once he peered inside the window? Just as he was straightening himself to look in, he heard voices, soft yet firm, like a bale of wheat ready to be rolled out.

'Thank you for doing this…' The voice was gruff.

Ajay's heart fell like a stone thrown into a deep well. There was a man in his daughter's room.

'It's the least I can do,' Pooja said quietly and steadily. 'It's for the cause.'

'Yes, I know that,' the man replied, 'but there are very few people, let alone a woman, who would risk everything to take us in.'

Pooja said something Ajay couldn't catch. The blood was thudding against his temples. He plastered his ear against the thin mud walls and strained to listen.

'Here, take this,' the man said. 'It is all I have and all I can give you right now. I insist.'

'Thank you,' his daughter replied and then paused. 'Is someone else coming tomorrow night?' she asked. Her tone was flat. It seemed natural—like she did this every day.

'Yes,' the man replied. 'You will have visitors all week long.'

There was a minute's silence before Ajay heard his daughter speak again, 'Do you know when *he* will come?'

'*He?*' the man asked, his voice puzzled.

'Yes, he,' Pooja said.

'Ah.' The man seemed to suddenly understand. 'It will be another ten days before he is back, so you can expect him then.'

Then, the conversation died down. There were the soft sounds of blankets rustling and the patter of feet, but after that, there was silence.

Ajay did not know how long he waited like that, outside his daughter's window, but when he finally left, he was a broken man.

His worst suspicions had been confirmed. His friends had been right.

His daughter, the apple of his eye, the forest angel, was nothing but a common prostitute.

It had been hours and yet nothing concrete had been achieved; no commitment given. He had repeated his story over and over again, and now, the words felt hollow on his tongue. He had signed papers, drunk the watery tea he was offered after his many pleas and had been shuffled off into the offices of three different officers. Ajay was tired. All he wanted was to leave the police station and go back home.

Home.

The very word made him sick to the stomach. The home he had lovingly built had been turned into a house of sacrilege and abomination and now he wanted justice to be served.

It had been ten days since the night Ajay had crouched under his daughter's window and learned the truth—the night his whole life came crashing down. Everything he had believed in had been muddied and trampled into the ground. After that night, he stood outside Pooja's room every night, and inevitably, he heard another man's voice, thanking his daughter for her services and giving her money for them.

He had been so revolted by the fact that this was going on in his home, right under his nose, and that his daughter had turned out to be the town whore, that he had lost his appetite and stopped praying in the mornings. He was consumed by it; it ate him up slowly and steadily from the inside out like a festering disease. On the sixth night, he could not take it any longer. As he lay in bed thinking of the unspeakable things that went on in his daughter's room, he grew cold.

He had had enough.

Damn the bitch, he thought bitterly. *Damn her to hell.*

That night, he made up his mind. He was going to expose her. He was going to ruin her like she had ruined him. He was going to go to the police and tell them everything.

Five hours later, Ajay was released by the officers. A plan had been set.

On the night of amavas, when the forest was plunged in darkness, the police would raid the hut and arrest the perpetrators. Prostitution was a serious crime, and without bail money, Pooja would languish in prison forever.

Ajay would be rid of the whore once and for all and he could finally die in peace.

If a passer-by were to be making his way through the forest on that moonless night, he would think nothing of it. Here was a forest, just like any other. One had to tread with caution because of the absence of moonlight, but otherwise it was just another forest. But they would not know that tonight, surrounding the perimeter of a farmer's hut, there were five policemen hidden in the foliage, waiting to make their move.

Hours flew by and then the forest finally stirred. A man appeared from the trees. He was tall, dark and covered in thick facial hair. He looked unwashed and his eyes darted suspiciously as he edged along the hut to Pooja's door. On his shoulder, there hung a heavy AK-47.

This was a new turn of events for the policemen, who watched even more carefully. They knew exactly who he was. He wasn't just a man looking for a night of pleasure. The man was a Naxalite. Suddenly, the stakes were very high.

Pooja's door opened a crack, and the man slipped in, looking behind him as he closed the door.

The policemen waited, then signalled to each other to

surround the hut. In the quiet of the night, as they approached her door, they could clearly hear Pooja's voice drifting towards them.

She was sobbing. 'I thought I'd never see you again. I thought you were dead.'

'I will never let anything happen to me before I see you, my love,' the man spoke. Thank you for taking in our comrades. Only you are brave enough to do it.'

'When will this stop?' she cried. 'This madness? When will this war stop?'

The man was quiet for a while, and then he spoke. 'When justice is delivered.'

The policemen were ready. In another moment, they broke down the door and found Pooja in the arms of a man known to be a Naxalite to police sources. They were naked and shocked at the intrusion.

'NO!' Pooja screamed, as she covered herself with a sheet. 'Take me but leave him alone.'

The man struggled against the police, but he had been outnumbered and handcuffs were slapped on both their wrists.

As the police dragged them into the jeeps waiting at the bottom of the hill, Ajay watched with his arms crossed. Tears stung his eyes, but he would not allow them to fall. When his daughter was a foot away from him, he went up to her and spat in her face, 'Whore!' he said, his voice breaking.

His daughter looked like a wild animal that had been cornered. Her hair was loose and free, her sari carelessly done, her chest heaving with sobs, and yet when she looked at her father, her face looked lost, like a child who was confused by the world, and this image broke Ajay's soul into smithereens.

'Father?' she croaked. Just as she was pushed into the police vehicle, realization dawned on her face. She looked back at him and screamed into the night.

'*Father!*'

3

The Tigress

The sun was setting over the horizon, painting the sky in a beautiful array of oranges and pinks. The air was still and the only sound that could be heard was the gentle rush of the river in the mangroves. Deep in the heart of West Bengal lay a sleepy little village called Bijoynagar; its name meant victory—victory over nature. Bijoynagar was home to a small population of farmers and their families who had been living there for generations. It was a peaceful place where the locals spent their days tending to their crops and livestock and gathered around the village well to chat and gossip. Evenings were spent around the fire, telling stories and singing traditional songs. The village was a haven of beauty and tranquillity, where time seemed to stand still. The locals were friendly and welcoming, and the atmosphere was one of contentment and joy. It was a reminder of a simpler time and of the beauty of India.

But this was no ordinary village. This was a village in the Sundarbans.

The Sundarbans is a vast mangrove forest located in the delta of the Ganges, Brahmaputra and Meghna Rivers in the Bay of Bengal. It is the largest mangrove forest in the world and is home to a variety of wildlife, including the Bengal tiger, saltwater crocodiles and the endangered Irrawaddy dolphins. A unique ecosystem, with its intricate network of rivers, creeks and estuaries, and its lush vegetation of mangrove trees—it is truly a place of mystery and beauty, where the sun sets over the horizon and the stars twinkle in the night sky. It is also a place of danger, where the Bengal tiger lurks in the shadows, the crocodiles roam in the waters while the Irrawaddy dolphins play in the waves and birds sing in the trees. Only a few in the village had explored the depths of the forest to uncover its vast secrets.

The night in the Sundarbans was alive with the sounds of tigers. The air was thick with the smell of the jungle. The moonlight illuminated the dense foliage of the mangrove forest, casting an eerie glow over the landscape. The trees were alive with the sounds of crickets and the occasional chirping of a bird. However, it was the deep, throaty roars of the tigers that dominated the night, echoing through the jungle. It was a sound that sent a chill down the spine of anyone who heard it. The tigers were out hunting and their calls were a reminder of the danger that lurked in the darkness. But the people of the Sundarbans were used to the sound and it was a comfort to them—it was a reminder of the beauty and power of nature. They knew that the tigers were a part of the ecosystem and they respected them. The nights were still and peaceful, punctuated by the occasional splash of a fish in the water heard from afar.

On one such night, as the village began to wind down, readying itself for a night of rest, a stranger found her way into it.

A cowherd had arrived late that evening, gathering his cattle from the grazing fields. The sun had set, and as he made his way on the paved path that led to the village, he scolded his cows. The village road at night was desolate and eerie. The snorts and moos of his cows and the occasional hoot of an owl in the distance echoed through the stillness. The road was lined with tall, gnarled trees that cast long, unsettling shadows across the path. The faint glimmer of stars in the night sky provided the only light. The air was still and heavy, with occasional rustle of leaves in the wind. It was a lonely, isolated place that seemed to stretch on forever, broken only by the occasional flicker of a distant street light. Just then, the cowherd saw something in the distance that made his heart stop.

It was a ghostly figure, dressed in a white sari, approaching him.

'Oh God, save me!' he yelled out, as he tried backing away, only to bump into one of his cows.

'Dada,' the ghostly apparition called out, 'please...I need help...'

The ghost speaks, the cowherd thought, his heart racing.

He had never believed in ghosts, but as it turned out, all those ghost stories he had once rubbished were true. He said his prayers, dreading the worst.

'Dada,' the woman said again, 'I am lost...can you please help me?'

She seemed to be glowing in the moonlight and he was mesmerized by her beauty. He felt a chill run down his spine as he approached her, but he was curious to find out who she was. The woman was now just a few feet away and the cowherd realized that this was no ghost but a widow who was lost. His heartbeat normalized, and gaining confidence, he straightened his back.

'Mashi,' he said, reluctantly, 'where do you want to go?'

'I am looking for the village of Bijoynagar,' she said.

'Oh,' the cowherd said, 'that is where I am heading. Come, I'll take you there.'

'Thank you so much,' the woman said. 'I will remember your kindness.'

The woman had nothing but a small suitcase, which looked light enough for her to carry without strain.

'If I may ask,' the cowherd began, 'what brings you to Bijoynagar so late at night?'

The woman sighed. 'It's a long story...but let me just tell you that the buses these days don't understand the concept of time any more,' she smiled.

The cowherd watched her as she spoke. She was a beautiful woman, with long, flowing dark hair. Her eyes were a deep, mysterious black, and her lips were a soft, rosy pink. She wore a simple white sari that seemed to shimmer in the moonlight, and her movements were graceful and ethereal. She seemed to float rather than walk and her presence was calming and peaceful. She was a vision of beauty and her presence was both captivating and haunting.

As they approached the sleepy village, the woman said, 'My name is Lalita, by the way, and I'm here to join the widow's commune since my husband passed away recently.'

'I am so sorry to hear that,' the cowherd said, his gaze drifting away from her face.

Lalita was a dusky beauty, five feet four inches tall with beautiful eyes that seemed to draw people in. Her hair was always in a neat braid and her skin was smooth and flawless. Everywhere she went, men wanted her. It wasn't easy being a widow, especially one with beauty. She often thought of her beauty as a curse instead of a blessing. As her feet stumbled through the dark, a memory resurfaced.

She recalled the incident like it was yesterday. She was walking home late one night after closing the tea shop she had been working at for the last few months when a man suddenly grabbed her from behind and dragged her into an alleyway. She was terrified and tried to scream, but he clamped his hand over her mouth and pinned her against the wall. In that moment, she felt completely helpless and powerless as he violated her. The fear and the shame she felt afterwards and the long journey to recovery were etched in her memory. Yet she also remembered the strength she found to speak out and seek justice, and the courage she found to move on and reclaim her life.

There was no justice or security for widows. They had no safety net. They were left to fend for themselves. Being a widow in an Indian village can be a difficult and lonely experience. Widows are often seen as a burden and are treated with less respect than other women. They are often excluded from social activities and may not be allowed to participate in religious ceremonies. They may also be expected to dress differently from other women. Widows may not be able to own property or have access to the same resources as other women. They may also be denied the right to remarry. Despite these challenges, many widows in Indian villages draw strength and resilience from their communities. They often receive support from their families and friends and derive solace from their faith.

After much suffering, Lalita had heard about a village in the Sundarbans where there existed a holistic commune for widows. It was distant from her past and provided the quietude necessary for a fresh start.

*A fresh start…*that's what she wanted the most.

Lalita's eyes lit up when they reached the village. The village at night time was a beautiful sight to behold. The stars shimmered in the sky and the moon cast a gentle glow over the village. The air was filled with the chirping of crickets and the occasional bark of a dog. The village was lit up by small oil lamps, casting a warm and inviting atmosphere. Amidst the quiet, there was the occasional chatter of villagers and the sound of laughter coming from the local tea shop. A scent of freshly cooked food drifted through the air, mingling with the fragrance of incense from the local temple. It was a peaceful and tranquil atmosphere, just what she was looking for.

'Where do I go from here?' Lalita asked the cowherd.

'I will take you to the commune because it is late, but you will have to meet the village elders tomorrow morning. Our widow commune is sacred and pure, and we will do everything in our power to keep it that way. The elders will verify your details and tell you whether you will be accepted into it,' he explained.

When he saw Lalita's face fall, the cowherd quickly clarified. 'Oh, it's only a formality, Mashi. Please don't worry.'

A few moments later, they arrived at a beautiful sprawling mud bungalow. Only a few lights flickered in the windows. The cowherd knocked on the door with his staff. 'Mashi… Mashi…' he called out, 'there's someone here to see you. Open the door.'

A minute later, they could hear footsteps approaching the mud floor. 'Just a minute, Ramlal, do you have to break my door down?'

The door opened with a creak and there stood an old woman. She was in her late sixties or seventies, thin and frail, with a wrinkled face and a stooped posture. Her skin was dark and her hair grey and thinning. She wore a white sari with a bright-coloured border and a white scarf draped over her head. On her nose, a gold nose pin shone. Her hands were wrinkled, while her fingernails were yellowed and brittle. Her eyes were sad and distant. She spoke in a soft, gentle voice, 'What is it, Ramlal? Why have you woken us up at this ungodly hour?'

Ramlal nodded gently in Lalita's direction. 'We have a new entrant, Mashi. She has come here to seek refuge. Perhaps you can host her for the night?'

The old woman had a suspicious look in her eyes as she assessed Lalita. She studied her from head to toe, her eyes lingering on the young woman's clothing and sparse jewellery. The old woman's mouth was set in a thin line and her brow was furrowed. She seemed to be trying to figure out Lalita's intentions as if she was trying to decide whether she was a threat or not. The old woman's gaze was intense and it was clear that she was not going to let the younger woman into the commune without a valid explanation.

'Why are you here?' the old woman asked Lalita.

'My husband was the love of my life. We had been married for over ten years and had a beautiful life together. He was always so kind and generous, and he was always there for me no matter what. But then one day, everything changed. He suddenly took ill with a mysterious illness. I rushed him to the hospital, but the doctor couldn't figure out what was wrong. He tried his best to save him, but it was too late. He passed away within a few days. I was devastated. I couldn't believe that he was gone. I felt like my life had been turned upside down. I was so lost without him. I felt like a part of me had died with him. I still can't believe that he's gone. It's been months since he passed away, but it still feels like it was just yesterday. I know that he's in a better place now and I'm thankful for the time we had together. But it still hurts. I feel the pain of his loss every single day. I know that I will never be the same again, but I'm trying to find a way to move forward and honour his memory. He will always be in my heart... I miss him so much. I miss his laugh, his smile, his kind words and his gentle touch...' Lalita's voice broke and she got teary-eyed as she said the words.

The old woman shuddered, her eyes glistening with tears. She had been moved by the story of the loss that Lalita had shared. She felt a deep sorrow for the pain that this young woman had gone through, empathizing with the grief that she carried. Having experienced her own losses in life, she knew how it felt to lose someone close to her and was deeply touched by the emotion that had been shared. The courage and strength shown in the face of adversity moved her. Grateful for the reminder of how precious life is and how quickly it can be taken away, she said, 'Come... Come inside. You must have had a very long journey, but now you have a home with us. Come... It will all be all right in no time. Life moves on and time is the only healer.'

She held Lalita by the arm and drew her into the commune.

'Thank you, Ramlal,' she said to the cowherd. 'Bid you a very good night.'

As the cowherd moved on, he noticed another light flicker to life in a window and it pleased him to know that the beautiful woman found refuge for the night.

The commune was built around a large courtyard bristling

with frangipani and jasmine shrubs, their fragrance perfuming the air.

'This is our home,' the old woman said, 'and my name is Kiran. I manage the daily running of our home. Come, I'll show you to your room. It's small but it has everything you need. I hope you will like it.'

The room lay at the end of the courtyard and contained a bed, a small stool and a cupboard for personal belongings. The window was shuttered. The old woman lit the oil lamp that sat on top of the cupboard. 'There...' she said, 'I will not keep you any longer because it is late and I'm sure you are heavy with sleep. Good night. I will come and see you in the morning and take you to the elders...' She paused. 'Oh, don't worry...it's just a formality.'

As the old woman left, gently closing the door behind her, Lalita thought about how it was the second time this night that she had heard that phrase. *Just a formality.* The mere mention made her heart race. What if this 'formality' revealed her secret, the one she had been holding so close to her chest for the past six months?

She sat down on the bed. There was nothing she could do about it anyway. If they found out, then so be it. If they didn't, this was truly a chance for a new beginning. She thought about changing into her night clothes, but exhaustion weighed heavily on her eyelids, and the minute she lay down on the musty sheets, she fell into a tired and deep sleep.

The morning sun shone brightly as the village elders gathered in the village square for their morning meeting. The village had been around for generations and the elders had been meeting for just as long. Among them were individuals of varying genders, all born and raised in the village with a deep understanding of its customs and traditions. The purpose of this morning's meeting was to discuss whether to allow the new widow into their village. The elders wanted to ensure that she would fit in and not disrupt the village's way of life. They began the meeting by discussing the widow's background, including her age, family and past experiences. They also delved into her current situation and the reasons for her arrival. Seated in a circle, each of them deeply contemplated the issue, debating the pros and cons of allowing the woman to stay. Some argued for her right to a safe place to live, while others expressed concerns that she might bring trouble to the village. After many hours of discussion and questioning Lalita, they reached a consensus: she would be allowed to stay, provided she followed the village's rules and respected the customs of the community.

'Welcome to Bijoynagar...' the oldest member of the council said, with a toothy smile. 'May it soon become your cherished home.'

A wave of relief washed over Lalita upon hearing the good news. Her heart had been pounding in anticipation all this time, and now that she had been accepted into the village, she could finally relax. Her shoulders dropped, her muscles loosened and her breathing slowed down. She had worried they would not grant it once they heard her husband's name and that she would be disappointed yet again. But now, a sense of joy and hope filled her, emotions she hadn't felt in a long time. She smiled, feeling the tension in her body melt away. She felt lighter, as if a heavy burden had been lifted from her shoulders. A sense of accomplishment surged through her, as though she had achieved something great. Lalita was also filled with gratitude for the good news. This was her fresh start and she was not going to let them down. She was also thankful for the courage she had found to keep going, even when things seemed impossible.

The council broke up and the daily life of Bijoynagar resumed.

Back in the commune, Lalita was determined to make something of her time there. Filled with a newfound sense of optimism, she was ready to face whatever the future held, knowing she could now move forward with confidence. She was ready to take on the world and make her dreams come true.

It didn't take long for the other widows in the commune to notice the hard work Lalita was putting in. She took on more responsibilities than required because she was determined to make a difference. Lalita was also a natural leader, willing to go above and beyond what was expected of her. A go-getter, she embraced risks and new challenges, putting in the extra effort to ensure her work was done to the best of her ability. She was not afraid to take on additional tasks and responsibilities or to ask for help when needed. She was organized and efficient and was always looking for ways to improve her work.

Very soon, Lalita began teaching classes at the commune, starting with singing and progressing to drawing and literature.

When she stood in front of the group of eager women, her eyes sparkled with enthusiasm and she had a commanding presence. She embodied a woman of knowledge, a teacher of the arts and literature. When she taught the other widows, Lalita pulled her long, dark hair into a bun, speaking with a strong and confident voice. She emphasized the importance of arts and literature in people's lives, illustrating their ability to inspire and empower women through the power of words, which serve as robust tools for expressing thoughts and feelings. She also spoke of the beauty of the written word, and how it could be crafted to create a world of their own.

Her singing classes became the most popular with almost all the widows attending.

Lalita stood in front of the room; her hands clasped in front of her. Her face was illuminated by a warm smile and her eyes filled with excitement. Though the women in the room were of different ages and backgrounds, they were all united in their desire to learn how to sing. They had gathered to learn from the woman who was an experienced singer and teacher. Lalita began the class by explaining its purpose, which was designed to help them learn how to sing in a way that was comfortable and enjoyable. She encouraged the women to introduce themselves and share why they had come to the class.

Lalita then began teaching the basics of singing, starting with proper breathing techniques. She demonstrated how to take a deep breath and exhale slowly, then asked the women to practise the technique. Moving on, she taught proper posture and how to use the diaphragm to support the voice. Next, she guided the women on how to warm up their voices. She explained the importance of warming up the vocal cords and demonstrated a few exercises to help the women do so. She then asked the women to practise the exercises.

Once their voices were warmed up, Lalita began teaching them how to sing. She covered topics such as pitch, rhythm and dynamics, asking them to practice singing simple melodies. She encouraged the women to experiment with different vocal techniques and discover their own unique sounds. Transitioning to harmonization, she explained the concept and demonstrated singing in harmony, then asked the women to practise singing in harmony with each other. Lalita concluded the class by having the women sing a familiar and enjoyable song together. The women sang with enthusiasm and joy, and Lalita smiled with pride as she watched them.

At the end of the class, Lalita thanked the women for their hard work and eagerness. She reminded them to practise what they had learned and encouraged them to keep singing.

Grateful for Lalita's guidance, the women thanked her and left the class feeling inspired and empowered.

Only a few months had passed before Lalita earned the nickname 'The Tigress' in the village. Fearless, confident and positive, everyone loved her optimism and selfless dedication towards the community and admired her courage. Her kindness extended to children and street animals. She was often found listening to others in despair, readily offering counsel and constantly prioritizing the needs of others above her own.

So it came as a shock when one summer morning a flurry of policemen rushed into the quiet village. As the sun began to rise, a police car pulled up into the village square and two officers stepped out of the car, making their way to the house of the village head. A few hours later, the council convened for an urgent and hushed meeting. The villagers knew something was up, but they could not guess what it was because there had been no crime or suspicious activity in their village in many years. In fact, the police only ever visited the village to collect bribes, which was usually a visit of half an hour or so. Daily life in the village came to a standstill as people gossiped in the tea shop or their homes about what tragedy could have befallen their community.

A few hours later, the police, escorted by a few village elders, emerged from the village head's hut and made their way to the widow commune.

They banged on the door. 'Mashi... Mashi...open up quick!' the chief police officer yelled.

The old woman opened the door, visibly anxious. 'What is it, Dada?' she asked, her brows knotted in concern.

'We have come to arrest a woman called Lalita,' the officer said.

The old woman gasped. 'Why? What for?'

'For murder!' the officer said belligerently. 'You have been harbouring a murderer all this time and now we've finally tracked her down.'

The old woman held her heart. 'The Tigress...how... she's not a murd—'

'It's okay, Mashi,' the officer continued seriously, 'we hear she's fooled the lot of you with her holier-than-thou act, but it's all over now.'

Before the old woman could respond, the policemen barged into the commune.

Lalita was in the commune's kitchen, assisting with lunch preparations, when she saw the police officers enter. Instantly, she knew the reason for their visit and her heart sank. The officers informed that they had a warrant for her arrest, charging her with the murder of her husband.

It all unfolded within minutes.

The officers handcuffed Lalita and escorted her out to the police car. Despite her fear and confusion, she was also determined to keep her grace.

She understood what she had done and why she had done it. She knew she was right.

On that fateful night many months ago, her husband raped and beat her, resulting in the loss of her unborn child. If she had not hit him back with the pressure cooker she would have died. She had only struck him in self-defence, but the steel of the cooker connected with her husband's temples and he fell to the ground with a groan, blood oozing out of his mouth and nose. He died instantly.

In a panicked state, Lalita left her abuser and fled the scene. She too was bleeding from the death of her unborn child, but she ran as fast as her broken body could carry her. To safety. *To a fresh start.*

The officers drove Lalita to the police station where she was placed in a holding cell. She was scared and cold but held her head high. Throughout the night, she grappled with fear and uncertainty about her fate.

The following morning, she was taken to court where she was formally charged with murder. Despite stating the circumstances surrounding the death of her husband and the fact that others had also seen the abuse she had suffered daily at his hands, Lalita was found guilty and sentenced to two years in prison. She was devastated and felt like her life was over. She had been an innocent woman, but was now paying the price for someone else's mistake.

During Lalita's two-year imprisonment, details about her past began to slowly circulate in Bijoynagar. People spoke of her husband as a monster, describing how he had been a drunkard and beat his wife every day. They recounted the tragic event when Lalita had miscarried her child that night. The tide began to turn. The villagers now longed for their Tigress to return.

When her sentence ended, the widows of the village eagerly awaited her release. Upon her stepping out of prison, they greeted Lalita with garlands and cheers, taking her back with them in tears of joy and warmth. Lalita was determined to move forward with her life and put this experience behind her. This time, she knew she was going to make a new beginning.

4

The Gift

*I*t is 4.30 a.m., that wonderful hour when the inky night begins to fade with the arrival of the sun. Despite the lingering darkness of the summer season, the air is cool.

Rohan wakes up in a dark room. The air is heavy with the snores of his sleeping family as he rubs the sleep out of his eyes. On the floor, on a thin bamboo mat, beside him his younger brother and sister lie curled up, sleeping. On the charpoy lies his mother. His father sleeps outside in these hot months. Moreover, there is no space for all of them in this heat.

Rohan would like to stay in bed a little longer, but he does not have that luxury. He turned eleven this year and his father decided it was time for his son to help him with their small business. Rohan would've liked to go to school or spend his time playing with the neighbourhood children, but he knows what he must do. He is mature enough to understand that they are poor and an extra pair of hands will help his father bring in more money. There are five mouths to feed and the extra help is much appreciated. Despite his young age, he has already faced many obstacles in life. He lives in poverty, and to help his family make ends meet, Rohan has taken on the responsibility of selling tea at the local school. Despite his circumstances, he is an intelligent and hard working boy with a passion for learning. He works hard to keep up with his earnings and dreams of one day going to school.

Rohan starts to get ready for the day. He steps out of their mud hut and heads to the outdoor bathroom, where he takes a cold water bath, shivering as he does so. As he gets dressed in his old but clean clothes, his father steps out of the hut. Once his father is dressed, they head out to the small tea stall that is set up near the village school.

They ride out together on the new Bajaj scooter his father bought a few months ago on a loan. The scooter is a blessing because it covers the kilometres from their house to the school in less than fifteen minutes. Otherwise, it used to take them forty-five minutes by cycle. Rohan sits at the back, his arms laden with the bags of tea, milk, sugar, ginger and other spices that they need for the day.

It is still early when they reach their spot under the shady banyan tree right across from Purulia Government School. It costs Rohan's father ₹500 every month to keep this spot. The local cops come and collect their 'rent' with their free cups of tea and biscuits in the first week of every month.

It is expensive but it is also prime real estate—proximity to the school means high footfalls and the shady banyan tree provides much relief in the sweltering summer months. The tree's branches spread wide, creating a large canopy of shade. Underneath the tree, Rohan's father has arranged his business for the day. A small table and two chairs are arranged in the shade's centre, with a large kettle of hot tea on one side. The tea stall owner has hung colourful paper lanterns from the branches of the tree, adding a festive touch to the area. Customers can sit underneath the tree and enjoy a cup of tea while they watch the hustle and bustle of the market. The banyan tree offers a peaceful place for these people to relax and enjoy the day.

The morning hours of Purulia Government School are quite lively and vibrant. As soon as the school bell rings, the buzz of students arriving can be heard. The tea stall is soon filled with students, teachers and other staff members, grabbing a quick cup of tea and a snack before the start of the school day. Rohan's father and Rohan are always ready with warm smiles and friendly conversation as they offer tea and snacks to the students and staff. It's a busy morning scene filled with the energy and enthusiasm of the students as they chat and laugh with each other and their teachers. Both father and son take great pride in their business and enjoy the company of their customers as they help to start off the school day on a positive note.

The arrival of the schoolchildren typically begins around 8 a.m. when the gates open and the students begin to file in.

They walk through the gates, some in groups, some alone, and make their way to the classrooms. Along the way, they greet the school staff and other students they recognize. As they enter their classrooms, they place their backpacks in the designated areas, pick up their books and take their seats. Class then begins and the students are eager to learn and engage with their teachers and peers.

Rohan stands in front of the school every day, selling tea and snacks to the students. He watches as they learn and grow, wishing he could be one of them. He is a bright, inquisitive boy who loves to learn, but he is unable to attend school due to his family's financial situation. He has a quiet, determined spirit that drives him to continue dreaming, despite the odds. He spends his days helping his family and the little extra money he earns from selling tea goes towards paying for his siblings' education. He is an optimist and he hopes that one day he will be able to attend school and achieve his dreams.

Purulia is a small village situated in the western part of the state, close to the borders of Jharkhand and Odisha. The village is home to several temples, including the famous Kalighat temple. It is also home to many rivers, including the Damodar and the Kangsabati. The city is known for its unique folk music, dance and art forms. The Chhau dance, a martial art form, is a popular attraction here. Agriculture is the main source of livelihood for most villagers and the area is known for its production of rice, pulses and other agricultural products. So there isn't much for Rohan to do without a formal school education. He will either have to go into farming or continue to run his father's business.

The maths teacher, Mr Biswas, stands in front of his class, hands on his hips and a deep frown on his face. He has been teaching for many years and has grown increasingly frustrated with the school syllabus. He feels that it does not adequately prepare students for the real world. He is particularly interested in experiential learning, where students can apply the concepts they learn in class to real-world situations.

He believes that this kind of learning is much more effective than rote memorization or theory alone. He is determined to make changes to the school syllabus and he is passionate about finding ways to make it more meaningful and engaging for his students.

He starts with something small, introducing a few new exercises and activities that require students to engage with the material in a practical way. He encourages students to think critically and apply their knowledge to solve problems. He is also eager to collaborate with other teachers to find ways to bring experiential learning into the classroom.

Experiential learning in maths is an approach to teaching and learning that focuses on hands-on, problem-based learning. It encourages students to take an active role in exploring and understanding mathematical concepts rather than relying solely on the traditional 'rote' approach of memorizing and repeating facts. This type of learning has many benefits, including a deeper understanding of mathematical concepts, better analytical and critical thinking, and enhanced creativity.

Examples of experiential learning in maths include 'real-world' problem-solving activities, such as designing a bridge from given materials and budget or creating a mathematical model to predict the outcome of a given situation. Other activities may involve researching a mathematical concept, such as the history of calculus or probability, or using online tools to explore a concept, such as using spreadsheets or graphing calculators to plot data.

Schools should favour experiential learning in maths because it engages students in the material, encouraging them to think critically and creatively. Furthermore, experiential learning can help to make maths more enjoyable and accessible to all students, regardless of their prior experience or ability.

One famous example of experiential learning in maths is the Maths Circles programme, which was developed by Soviet mathematician Boris Delaunay in the 1920s. This programme encouraged students to engage in mathematical conversations and activities in a small group setting and it was adopted by many schools across the Soviet Union. Another example is the Maths Busking programme, developed by mathematician and educator Timothy Gowers. This programme encouraged students to explore mathematics through an interactive performance, using music and props to explain mathematical concepts in an engaging way.

Mr Biswas has been talking to the faculty at length about his ideas, but they are hesitant to embrace this approach. One day, frustrated with his daily debates with other teachers in the staffroom, Mr Biswas decides to have his tea outside instead of in the staffroom. He storms out of the school gates and makes his way across the road. The tea stall is busy serving the rickshaw drivers and a few ladies stopping to have a cup of tea before continuing with their day. Soon a chair is free and Mr Biswas quickly takes it and asks for a cup of tea and a biscuit.

Nearby, a boy is talking to a man, a kettle in his hand. They seem to be having a minor argument over change.

'I'm telling you it's 72, Dada,' the boy says firmly.

'You're very quick to come to that number without even thinking. How do I know you're not cheating me, huh? Let me calculate it myself,' the older man says. 'If you are wrong, I will keep five bucks. That will serve you a lesson for being so cocksure with your elders.'

'Sure,' says Rohan, looking a little amused. 'And if I win, you will have to give me ten bucks extra.'

'Ten! What do you think I am?' the man says, 'A bank?'

'Okay, five then, Dada!' Rohan says. 'A bet is a bet.'

'Go on…Mr Sharma,' Rohan's father says with a smile, 'but be warned…our Rohan here is very good with adding and subtracting. He is like a human calculator.'

The old man frowns as he begins to work out the figure. After a while of calculating and recalculating, he scowls. 'It's 72.'

Rohan sticks out his hand with a smile.

'Here…keep your five bucks,' the man says, and then turning to Rohan's father continues, 'These young children are full of tricks, I say.'

Rohan's father laughs. 'I warned you, Mr Sharma. He's good at this. He keeps the accounts at home these days.'

When Rohan comes to pour Mr Biswas his cup of tea, the maths teacher says, 'So are you good with multiplication too?'

'I guess,' Rohan says softly.

'How did you learn?'

'I don't know…' Rohan says. 'It just comes naturally to me.'

'Do you want to do a short quiz?' Mr Biswas asks.

Rohan looks at his father.

'I'll give you fifty bucks if you get it all right…' the maths teacher says.

Rohan's father says, 'Fifty bucks! Rohan, you better get it all right!'

'Okay,' Rohan says with a smile. 'Go on.'

Mr Biswas takes a moment to compose himself before he begins. 'What is 7 times 9?'

'63,' comes the reply from Rohan.

'What is 15 times 17?'

'255.'

'48 times 92?'

'4,416.'

'118 into 654?'

Rohan takes a moment. His eyes are focused on the

ground and then he replies, '77,172.'

Mr Biswas has forgotten the tea he is holding in his hand. 'That is exceptional! What is your name, boy?'

'Rohan...'

'Okay, Rohan, do you want to try another type of question?'

'That's not fair,' Rohan replies.

'No...no,' Mr Biswas says. He reaches into his pocket, pulls out his wallet and takes out a ₹50 note. He gives Rohan the money. 'You have rightly won this. However, I'm just curious to know how you will answer the next question... it's just one question... why don't you give it a try, but only if it interests you.'

'Okay, why not!' Rohan says. 'There aren't that many customers right now anyway.'

Mr Biswas puts down his cup of tea on the bench and rubs his hands. There is a gleam in his eyes. 'Okay, Rohan... here is a puzzle. Think about it carefully and then give me your answer, okay?'

'Okay,' says Rohan.

'Here we go...What do you get if we have 4x + 5 when x = 3?'

Rohan takes a moment to think about it. Aloud, he says, 'If x is 3...'

Mr Biswas watches the boy carefully.

A minute later, Rohan says, '17...'

Mr Biswas licks his lips.

'Am I right?' Rohan asks.

'My boy…yes. You are right! But how did you get to the answer?'

'So, given, $4x + 5$. Now if I put $x=3$, I get: $4(3) + 5 = 12 + 5 = 17$.'

'Yes, yes!' Mr Biswas says enthusiastically. He almost wants to clap. 'How old are you, Rohan?'

'Eleven,' Rohan replies.

'Wonderful…just wonderful…' Mr Biswas mutters under his breath. This encounter has recharged him more than the cup of tea could ever have. An idea strikes him at that moment. 'Would you be open to doing some classes with me in your free time?' He turns to Rohan's father. 'Your boy is a genius at maths. I think he should definitely have some lessons and I will be happy to teach him.'

Rohan's father looks at the maths teacher in puzzlement. 'Sir, we are but poor folk who need all hands on deck to make a living. I cannot afford Rohan's absence during our work hours and neither do I have the money to pay for lessons. If I did, I would have sent him there,' he says, pointing at the school across the road.

'No…no, sir,' Mr Biswas says. 'There is no need to pay me. You have no idea how difficult it is to find a student like your son. He is bright and will have a successful future if he starts now and works on his gift. Yes, he has a gift. I have been teaching for over twenty years now and I have never come across a child this bright. I won't take up too much of his time. An hour a day after school and when you are done with your work is all I ask. We can study right here…after which I will drop Rohan home. Does that work?'

Rohan's father and Rohan exchange a look, and then the father tells the teacher, 'I will have to think about it, Mr…'

'Mr Biswas…' the maths teacher says. 'Fair enough. I will come here tomorrow during lunch hour if you would like to tell me then.'

And with that, Mr Biswas pays for his cup of tea and heads back to school. He is absolutely delighted with his discovery of this brilliant 11-year-old boy who is so good at mental maths. After teaching for twenty years, he has never encountered such a remarkable student and is filled with admiration for the boy's talent. He is amazed that Rohan has no prior education, yet can solve complex mathematical problems with ease. He is also proud of the boy's humble beginnings as the son of a tea seller and is determined to nurture Rohan's natural gift and help him reach his full potential. Mr Biswas is inspired and energized by Rohan's ability to think outside the box and is eager to see the heights to which he can reach with his talent. He hopes that Rohan's father will agree to the lessons for his son.

The room is dark and quiet, with the only light coming from the streetlamp outside. Rohan's father is in bed, eyes closed, but his mind is wide awake. He thinks of the maths teacher's offer to teach his son for free. He knows his son is smart and he wants him to have the best education possible.

But he is also worried about the consequences of this offer. Would this education set Rohan up for failure later in life? He doesn't have the money to pay for a proper education, so what would happen when Rohan's free lessons ran out? Would he be so encouraged by these lessons that he will feel let down and disappointed when he can't continue them?

Rohan's father sighs heavily, worrying about his son's future. He wants to do what is best for him, but he also has to consider the practicalities of the situation. He thinks of the look on Rohan's face when he is excited about learning something new. He remembers the way Rohan's eyes light up with curiosity and how eager he is to try something new. He knows that this can be a great opportunity for Rohan, but he is also aware that there is a risk involved.

Rohan's father closes his eyes and says a silent prayer for his son. He asks for guidance and strength for his family and for Rohan to find success and happiness in whatever path he chooses. He then makes a silent vow to always do his best to provide for his son, no matter what. With a heavy heart, Rohan's father drifts off to sleep.

The sun is setting, casting a golden hue on the sky as the school day draws to a close. Mr Biswas is making his way to the tea seller's stall. He has been invited by Rohan's father to give the boy free maths lessons in the evenings and he is filled with a sense of excitement and anticipation.

As he arrives, he sees Rohan already waiting for him under the banyan tree. Mr Biswas smiles and waves, and Rohan smiles back, standing up to greet his teacher.

Mr Biswas begins by introducing a new concept of experiential learning. He asks Rohan to imagine a situation and then explains how he will solve the problem. This is followed by some maths problems for Rohan to solve.

1. If a store has 8 blue pencils, 5 yellow pencils and 3 green pencils, how many pencils are there in total?
2. If a bus is travelling at a speed of 70 km per hour, how long will it take to travel a distance of 210 km?
3. If a rectangle has a length of 8 cm and a width of 6 cm, what is the area of the rectangle?

After Rohan answers these questions, Mr Biwas explains a few maths concepts to the boy during his first lesson.

As the weeks fly by, Rohan gets better and better at solving problems and Mr Biwas begins challenging him with more difficult problems.

'So Rohan, today we will be reviewing some difficult maths problems. Don't get scared. They are based on yesterday's concepts and you should be able to crack them in no time.'

'Okay, sir, let's get started.'

'Good! I like your enthusiasm. Let's start with problem number one. Solve for x: $3x + 6 = 24$.'

Rohan thinks for a minute. 'Hmmm, let me see... I think the answer is $x = 6$.'

'Excellent!' Mr Biswas exclaims. 'You are right. Now let's try problem number two. Find the circumference of a circle with a radius of 12.'

Rohan thinks again. 'I think the answer is 75.36.'

'Very good!' Mr Biswas says. 'You got that exactly right. Finally, let's try problem number three. Find the area of a triangle with sides of length 8, 6 and 10.'

'I think the answer is 24. Am I right?' says Rohan.

'Excellent work, Rohan!' says Mr Biwas. 'You've really been improving. Keep up the great work!'

Rohan is a quick learner and is able to answer all the questions correctly. Mr Biswas is happy to see Rohan's enthusiasm and dedication. After the lesson, they both return to their respective homes, feeling fulfilled after a day of learning.

The weeks become months, and with each passing day, Mr Biwas grows even more confident about his theory that experiential learning is the only way to go. He wants to change the syllabi of the school so that they lean more heavily towards experiential learning. In fact, he has been working on a syllabus for the Purulia school for many months. He has made many drafts and the final one seems perfect to him. He has a meeting with the board tomorrow to discuss the proposal. He is both nervous and excited about the meeting.

Mr Biswas stands in front of the board of directors with his proposal in hand. He begins to explain his syllabus.

'Good morning, everyone,' Mr Biswas begins. 'Thank you for having me here today. I've been working on an experiential learning maths syllabus for our school and I'd like to share it with you. I believe that the current maths curriculum is outdated and not very engaging for our students,' he says. 'My syllabus focuses on students understanding the concepts through hands-on experience, rather than memorization. It involves hands-on activities, student-led projects and a focus on the application of maths concepts. I think it will really inspire our students and help them understand maths better.'

He goes on to explain the details of his syllabus, which includes activities such as field trips and classroom experiments. He can see the board members become more and more interested as he goes on. When he finishes, he looks around the room, expecting to see approval on the board members' faces. But instead, he sees doubt.

'This is a very drastic change,' one board member says. 'The teachers' union is sure to oppose it and it will be difficult to get them to agree.'

The other board members nod in agreement.

'I understand your concern,' Mr Biswas says, 'but I think this is something that will benefit the students greatly. I have been working with a boy for the past few months, his name is Rohan. He is a tea seller's son with no prior education yet he has shown me that experiential learning can do wonders. Rohan can solve complex maths problems that are taught only in the senior classes. He is literally miles ahead of the average student. Okay, I have to admit, he is very bright naturally but our lessons have honed his skills faster and better. Imagine how well our school children will fare if we introduced this concept into everyday learning!'

The board members look at each other, clearly conflicted. After what seems like an eternity, they finally speak.

'We appreciate your proposal, Mr Biswas,' the board chair says, 'but we're going to have to decline. This is a drastic change and I'm not sure it's the best option for our school.'

Mr Biswas can't believe it. After all his hard work, his proposal had been rejected.

'I think the benefits of this syllabus will outweigh any resistance we may face. I believe it will really revolutionize the way our students learn maths,' says Mr Biswas.

'We appreciate your enthusiasm,' says a board member, 'but we just don't think it's right for our school.'

Mr Biswas takes a moment to gather his thoughts. His heart is racing like a bullet train. He is angry. The board has refused to even think about this. This whole meeting has been a sham—an administrative tick mark that they can later pull out as evidence to say but we did hear him out at least.

'I see,' Mr Biswas finally says through gritted teeth. 'Well, thank you for hearing me out.'

And with that, he storms out of the boardroom, his head spinning.

The evening sun is beginning to set as Mr Biswas paces back and forth in his office, his hands clasped behind his back. His face is contorted with anger, given the fact that he has just been informed that the school board rejected his proposal for a new maths syllabus. He had worked tirelessly on this syllabus but it was all for nought.

He reflects on the resistance to change, how everyone seems content in their comfort zones and how there's a reluctance to explore application-based learning. Despite this, he firmly believes in the potential of his students and is certain that this syllabus will help them reach their full potential.

Just then Mr Biswas has an idea. He picks up the newspaper and scans its contents again. He stops at an article he had just read about the chief minister visiting Purulia in a few weeks. He is sure that this is the perfect opportunity to present his revised syllabus to the chief minister. This is his final shot and he is going to grab the opportunity.

Mr Biswas is ecstatic when he opens the email from the chief minister's office. For the past few days, he has been writing emails, outlining his proposal and requesting an appointment with the chief minister. Knowing the minister's interest in progressive education models, he feels this is his best chance.

Quickly, he prints out the proposal he has been working on and puts it into a folder. He also puts together some visual aids to help him explain the details of the proposal better. He is excited to be able to present his idea to the chief minister and hopefully get it approved.

The next day, Mr Biswas makes his way to the chief minister's office. He is dressed in a crisp white shirt and a grey suit. He is nervous but also excited. As he enters the building, he is greeted by a secretary who ushers him into the chief minister's office.

The meeting room is small and sparsely decorated. Mr Biswas is nervous, his palms sweating as he waits for the chief minister to arrive. Fifteen minutes later, as she enters the room, Mr Biswas notices her smaller stature compared to the photographs he has seen, but her intense gaze commands attention. Her presence is intimidating, and he can tell she will not take any nonsense. She has been the chief minister of West Bengal for the last decade and has a reputation for being a strong leader.

Mr Biswas begins his presentation without much hesitation, outlining his proposal to reform the school system by starting with the syllabi. She listens to it intently as he details the benefits of the revised syllabus, accompanied by the visual aids he has prepared to help explain the concepts better.

When he concludes his presentation, she speaks. Her voice is strong and she is clear and direct. She tells him that although his proposal has merit, it will not work. She cites potential opposition from the teachers' union that has been in place for a long time and they would be angry at the suggestion of change.

'The school system is already working, so why should it be changed?' she says. 'Why fix something that isn't broken?'

Mr Biswas is deflated. He had hoped his idea would be well received, but it isn't. He thanks the chief minister for her time and exits the room with a heavy heart.

That evening, Mr Biswas sits at home nursing a drink, his mind spinning with ideas. He can't believe the chief minister rejected his proposal after he had poured so much care and effort into it. His thoughts drift to his student, Rohan. He had seen so much potential in the boy and been so proud of his progress.

He picks up the phone, aimlessly scrolling through the news and social media. Suddenly, he gets an idea: he could start a YouTube channel to share educational content. He could start with basic maths modules and make them accessible to everyone. He could even rope in Rohan and make him lead the classes.

Taking a deep breath to steady himself, he quickly calls Rohan's father to explain the situation. He highlights the potential of the YouTube channel as a platform for sharing learning content. He explains that Rohan could take the lead in the classes, which would help him hone his skills in the process.

Rohan's father is hesitant at first but then agrees, after hearing the enthusiasm in Mr Biswas' voice. He expresses gratitude for his belief in Rohan and assures him that he will help with the channel in any way he can.

Mr Biswas hangs up, feeling a little less dejected and

with a newfound determination. He smiles, knowing he has made the right decision.

⚭

The process of launching the channel takes months to materialize. Mr Biswas and Rohan spend a lot of time talking about ideas and the modules they would like to present. Also, the first hurdle is to decide on a name for the channel. After much deliberation, they settle on 'Easy Learning', aiming to ensure that the channel is accessible to everyone, regardless of their background or level of knowledge.

The next challenge is generating content for the channel. They decide that Mr Biswas will shoot the videos where Rohan explains concepts, while Rohan will film Mr Biswas teaching others.

They start shooting the videos late at night as Rohan still has to get up early the next day to help his father. This proves challenging as both are exhausted by the end of the day. In order to make the videos more dynamic, they try out different camera angles and experiment with the editing process. They also learn how to use different editing software, which is a difficult and time-consuming process, but they eventually get the hang of it.

Finally, they upload the videos to the channel. This is a difficult task as they have to make sure that the videos are aesthetically pleasing, as well as making sure that the audio and visuals are of high quality.

Overall, setting up the channel is a learning experience. They learn how to work together, navigate different software tools and optimize the channel's appeal to viewers. By the end of it, they have created a platform that is sure to attract a wide audience.

It is a bright and sunny day in the small town. On its outskirts is a small house where Rohan and Mr Biswas are hard at work. The two have invested all their time and energy into creating the YouTube channel called Easy Learning.

They've worked tirelessly over the past few weeks, and their hard work has finally paid off. The channel has gained its first subscribers and word is slowly beginning to spread. People have started engaging with their content and the pair are beginning to tweak their new videos based on the suggestions of their subscribers.

Day in and day out, Rohan and Mr Biswas continue to work hard, and slowly but surely, their channel gains more and more subscribers. In three months, they reach ten thousand subscribers, and their influence becomes more widespread. Their videos start to go viral and their subscriber count keeps climbing.

A year later, Easy Learning boasts a million subscribers and their channel has also become profitable. The channel is now Rohan's full-time job. He is able to provide for his family who are incredibly proud of him and his success.

They've even purchased a car and a small house. Rohan's siblings now attend school.

Together, they have achieved something extraordinary.

The atmosphere is electric at the Easy Learning office. Mr Biswas and Rohan are beaming with delight as they have just been contacted by an angel investor who wants to fund their enterprise and take it to the next level.

The duo has worked hard for months, brainstorming ideas, creating videos and marketing the channel to grow their viewership. Now, their efforts are being rewarded. Newspapers and popular online journals have started featuring their success story, and the angel investor wants to seize the opportunity and invest in the growing channel.

Mr Biswas and Rohan hug each other and jump around with joy and relief. They are overwhelmed; they can't believe that their dream is finally coming true. This is the beginning of a new era for them, and they are filled with optimism, eager to see what the future has in store. It is a momentous day, one that they will remember and cherish for the rest of their lives. They took a huge risk in starting the channel, but it has paid off, and now their dream of changing the world, one video at a time, is becoming a reality.

The office of the chief minister of West Bengal is abuzz with activity as the news of Easy Learning's success spreads. Mr Biswas and Rohan, the two masterminds behind the popular YouTube channel, are both ecstatic. They are in the middle of celebrating their success when their phones begin to ring. They are both surprised to hear the voice of the chief minister on the other end of the line. She congratulates them on their success and expresses an interest in meeting them to discuss their techniques and how they could be applied to upgrade the school syllabi in the region.

Mr Biswas and Rohan are both overwhelmed by this invitation. After a few moments of stunned silence, they accept and make arrangements to travel to the chief minister's office.

When they arrive, they are welcomed warmly by the staff and ushered into the chief minister's office. The chief minister offers them a seat and thanks them for coming. She then begins to explain her vision of using the Easy Learning technique to upgrade the school syllabi in the region. She believes that this will help create a more accessible and effective form of education, benefiting the students of West Bengal.

The duo are thrilled at the prospect of their work having such an impact. They thank the chief minister for the opportunity and promise to do their best to make her vision a reality. After a few more words of encouragement, the chief minister thanks them for their time and bids them farewell.

Mr Biswas and Rohan leave the office feeling a mixture of pride, joy and satisfaction. Their dream has become a reality and they are now presented with an opportunity to make a real difference in the lives of the people in West Bengal. They head out with a newfound sense of purpose and determination.

5

Test Drive

*A*mit Ghose stood on the balcony, his hands resting on the balustrade, as he took in the view of the surrounding area. His flat was on the eighth floor, affording him a spectacular view of Salt Lake, all the way to the main highway. The wind was always high here due to the elevation, but he didn't mind. Kolkata could get very muggy and humid during the summer months and this wind provided much respite without hiking up the electricity bills. As the wind whipped through his hair and his crumpled kurta, Amit observed the society compound. Below, he could see children playing in the park and a few elderly people taking a walk in the thoughtfully constructed walking zones around the entire society. These walking paths were made of astroturf with railings on both sides. The surface was soft on the knees of the elderly and the railings were useful in case someone slipped or simply got tired and wanted to take a break.

It was this aspect—the thoughtfully planned and intelligent design of the society, called Green Views, that had first caught Amit's attention. As a product designer who had graduated from the National Institute of Design in Mumbai, design mattered to him and his wife. They had met each other on the campus and soon fell in love because they shared similar values about life, how they should live, and their philosophies about renewable resources, sustainable design and living in harmony with nature. They were both sticklers for recycling and lived rather frugally. They never shopped on the high street and avoided fast fashion and products that were plastic-dominant. In fact, even in their eighth-floor flat, on the balcony adjoining their kitchen, the couple had set up a three-tier composting system for their kitchen waste.

Rupa first learned about Green Views when she stumbled upon a brochure of the property at an office event. She might have overlooked it if the brochure hadn't been printed on hemp paper. Given that it was not cheap printing on hemp paper, she concluded that whoever made this decision had gone to great lengths and taken meticulous care to distinguish these brochures. She immediately recognized the care for the environment behind it. She took a copy of the brochure home and showed it to Amit. They spent a considerable amount of time reading and studying it. Green Views seemed ahead of its time; there was certainly no other place like it in central Kolkata. The society offered solar-powered options for flat owners and renters. Additionally, all common spaces, including the gym, indoor pool area, squash courts, parks, community centres and amphitheatre, were solar-powered. There was also a strict waste segregation system that all the residents in the society had to maintain and adhere to. Furthermore, there was also a large composting area that converted leaf litter and other organic matter into rich vermicompost that could once again be used in the gardens and parks within the complex. All the trees and other flora were indigenous.

Rupa, who worked as a landscaping designer, was especially delighted by this, because she despised 'green concrete'—trees and plants like palms and water tupelo that required large amounts of water to survive, did not enrich the soil and were purely there for aesthetic reasons. Green concrete was very common, found in almost all living complexes, public avenues and corporate offices. However, it served no purpose. Rupa loved working with indigenous plants that organically followed the natural seasonal cycles, giving back to the soil and people. The silk cotton tree was one such example. In spring, it produced beautiful waxy large-petalled flowers that turned into seeds, releasing great quantities of cotton, which people gathered to make pillows and mattresses. These indigenous trees also attracted a variety of birds and insects drawn to their unique features. Thus, these trees kept the natural and local cycle of life running beautifully.

By the end of the evening, Amit and Rupa were both convinced that this was the place they wanted to live in and potentially raise a family in the future. The next day, Amit called the number provided in the brochure and had a long conversation with the sales representative, who asked them to come in for a meeting at their office, after which they would be taken on a tour of the property. A week later, on a Saturday, Amit and Rupa made their way from their central Kolkata location to Green Views. The sales representative ran through the highlights of the campus' features and benefits, taking them both on an exhaustive walk around the premises. By the end of the tour, Amit and Rupa were sold. They held each other's hands tightly. In the office, they discussed prices over a cup of tea, only to realize that the place was way beyond what they could afford. Their hearts sank. Nevertheless, they left behind their visiting cards before leaving the campus.

On the way back home, Amit did some basic maths while Rupa drove. 'Renting, even though our rent is pretty high, is more affordable than a flat in Green Views,' he remarked.

Rupa sighed. 'It was a nice place though. At least we had a look around. It gave me some ideas for work.'

A month later, Amit received a call from the sales representative they had met at Green Views, informing them that there was a distress sale of a two-bedroom flat, as the owner had to leave the country due to urgent personal business. Amit enquired about the price of the flat. When the sales representative revealed the amount, Amit could barely believe his ears. The flat was now selling for half its original value. While the sum was still relatively high for them, it seemed manageable. He hung up, informing the representative that he would discuss it with his wife and return with a response. That evening, Rupa and Amit decided to buy the place. They knew they would be paying EMIs for the next 20 years, but they believed it would be worth it.

'What are you daydreaming about?' Rupa asked as she stepped on to the balcony, a cup of tea in her hand.

'Nothing,' Amit replied, turning to his wife. 'Actually, I was just thinking about how lucky we were to get this place.'

'Yes,' she agreed, sitting down beside him. 'I thank our lucky stars every day. I never take it for granted. I mean, just look at this view.'

They both stood silently on the balcony as the wind ran through the wind chimes Rupa had hung from the ceiling. The sky was a bright blue with big, fluffy clouds strewn across it.

'Right,' Amit said, getting up. 'I suppose I should change. We must get going in an hour.'

'Okay,' replied Rupa. 'I am kind of excited by this.'

'Yeah,' said Amit, as he stepped into the living room. 'That car of ours really needs an upgrade.'

Two hours later, Amit and Rupa pulled into the Voltaus showroom, not far from their home in the eastern part of Kolkata. As they parked their car, they noticed that the interior of the showroom seemed pretty dark.

'Are they closed?' Rupa said.

'I checked their website. It said they were open on Saturdays,' Amit replied.

'Let's go check it out anyway. If they are closed, we'll come back another day,' Rupa proposed.

They got out of their car and walked to the showroom. As they neared the door, they found it wasn't closed; there were people and sales representatives inside. The showroom windows were coated with a film that made it appear dark from the outside. Amit noted that this type of window film helped keep buildings cooler in the brutal summers. It was pretty cool, he thought.

'Welcome to Voltaus,' a young man greeted them. 'How can I help you today?'

'Hello,' said Amit. 'We've come to look at a car. Our old one is giving up on us and we want to switch to an electric model because we both believe that is the future.'

'You've come to the right place, then. My name is Rahul. It's nice to meet you both,' Rahul said, shaking hands with them. 'Please come into my office and let's talk about what you are looking for and what models might be suitable for your needs.'

'Do you mind if we just take a look around? You could tell us the model's USPs as we view them?' Rupa asked.

'Sure! We can totally do that,' Rahul said. Another man approached them, holding a tray with two glasses of water. Rupa took one.

'Can I get you a coffee, tea or some fresh juice?' the man offered.

'No, no...' Amit refused, 'thank you so much, we're okay.'

'Okay then,' Rahul said. 'Let's begin.'

They started from the back of the showroom with the original models of the company. Rahul walked them through the vehicle's specifications, special features and mileage. After looking at four or five models, they stopped in front of a hatchback.

'And this is the Voltaus 203—our latest and best car. Fully electric. It's the most updated model with up to 250 hp. The 194 hp front-wheel-drive model will get up to 57 mpg combined. Its 19 inch wheels are designed to maximize range with minimal mass and low coefficient drag, equipped with all-season tyres for enhanced handling and versatility in most road and weather conditions. It has a sunroof and extra-large boot space, and just look at its interiors.' Rahul opened the door. 'Luxury eco-leather seats with carbon oak trim. And the speakers in this car are amazing, Bose. The car will be ready by morning when you charge it overnight. And by the way, there are charging stations for Voltaus across the country.'

Amit and Rupa peered inside the car. 'It looks good,' Amit remarked.

'Would you like to take it out for a ride?' Rahul offered.

Amit and Rupa exchanged a look. 'Why not?' Rupa agreed.

'That's great. Just give me a minute, I'll be back,' Rahul said.

'It's such a slick-looking car!' Rupa exclaimed softly to her husband, barely able to contain her excitement.

'Yes. This is the one, Rupa!' he affirmed, squeezing her hand.

Rahul returned with a manual for the couple. 'Let's take it out!' He smiled at them. 'Who wants to drive?'

Rupa turned to Amit, 'You go for it.'

Amit nodded.

'Okay,' Rahul said, as he handed Amit the key. 'Let me run you through a few things. It's very simple—you will get the hang of it in no time.'

Rupa sat at the back, running her hands over the seats. She liked the fact that they were imitation leather but still felt smooth and soft. Taking a deep breath, she savoured the new car smell. In the front seat, Rahul explained the basics.

Sometime later, they were on their way. Amit drove slowly, taking in the new information and getting a feel of the machine. In a few moments they were out of the narrow street that led to the showroom and out on the open highway. Rahul explained the various features of the car while Amit sailed steadily along the smooth roads in the eastern part of Kolkata.

While Rupa looked out of the car window, Amit tried to get comfortable in the driver's seat. He had been driving his whole life, starting at thirteen when his father taught him how to drive their sedan. Driving was second nature to him, so it didn't take him long to get the hang of this car. Even though it was fully electric, the basics remained the same. But no matter how much he shifted his weight, adjusted the seat or tried a different grip on the steering wheel, he couldn't seem to get comfortable.

There were a few things that struck him as he drove.

There was a strange buzzing in his ear—a sound he had never heard before. His stomach felt uneasy, as if he had eaten a bad meal at a restaurant. But both Rupa and he had just grabbed a very light breakfast, toast and tea, before they had set out for the showroom. A few minutes later, he could no longer hear what Rahul was telling them. He felt his heartbeat quicken and he could hear it in his ears. Sweat broke out all over his face, his armpits grew damp, and soon, his whole shirt was drenched.

Rahul noticed this and asked, 'Are you feeling hot, sir?'

'No...yes...I...' Amit couldn't quite find the words to explain the deep unease bubbling up inside him.

'I'll just turn up the AC to max...' Rahul said, pressing a button on the dashboard's digital screen.

'God, it's freezing in here...' Rupa remarked. 'Do we really need it so high?'

'Sir is feeling hot,' Rahul explained.

Rupa turned to look at her husband. Sweat was now streaming down his face, and he looked pale, his hands trembling on the wheel. 'Amit, are you okay? You don't look too well,' she said, reaching out to touch his forehead. 'You don't seem to have a fever... What's wrong?'

'I'm fine, really,' he said curtly.

There was a moment's awkward silence in the car.

'I'm sorry. I don't know. I'm not unwell. Perhaps I ate something that didn't suit me yesterday,' he said.

Rahul resumed speaking about the features of the car, but his words fell on deaf ears. The buzzing sound had returned and Amit's unease increased. He knew he wasn't unwell; he had eaten nothing dodgy the day before, only the tiffin Rupa packed for them both and ate nothing else at the office or after either. There was something not right about this car. That's what it was, Amit realized. He had never felt so uncomfortable and frightened while driving in all these years. Heck, he had even driven a tractor once in Ludhiana and had been fine. There was something very strange about this particular car and he seemed to be reacting physically to it.

In the back seat, Rupa sensed that her husband was deep in thought. After all these years together, she could read him like a book. It was also odd to see him like this. Amit was usually calm and collected. He wasn't unwell, so what could it be? Whatever was bothering him was new and significant because she had never seen him so anxious.

'Rahul, we've had a lovely drive. I think we should call it a day. It truly is a fantastic car,' Rupa intervened.

'Done already?' Rahul looked at her through the mirror.

Rupa glanced at her husband, who seemed to be wrestling with something in his mind. 'Yes, I think we are done. Why don't we head back now?'

Amit did not hear his wife. It was only when Rupa gently touched his arm that he snapped out of the feeling that had gripped him. 'Yes?' he asked her.

'Let's go back, Amit,' she said firmly.

'Yes, yes…' Amit said absent-mindedly.

They drove back home in silence. Amit looked better— he had stopped sweating and his hands were steady on the wheel. In their apartment, Rupa made two cups of coffee and gave one to her husband, who had seated himself on the living room balcony.

They sat in silence for a while, listening to the wind gently stirring the wind chimes. Then Rupa spoke, 'What happened today?'

Amit did not reply.

'Are you feeling unwell?'

'No,' Amit said softly. 'I am fine.'

'So what happened then? Because you didn't look well at all. Should we get your blood pressure checked?' she asked with concern.

'No, Rupa, I'm really fine,' Amit said. 'It's just that…'

'What?' she prompted.

'I don't know how to explain it…' Amit hesitated.

'You can try?' Rupa encouraged.

'There was something…not right about the car,' Amit confessed, turning to his wife.

Rupa raised an eyebrow.

'See…I knew you would think it's crazy.'

'I didn't say anything!' she protested.

They fell silent.

'What was wrong with the car, Amit?' Rupa enquired after a while.

'I don't know,' Amit began. 'I've been thinking about this since we left the showroom. There's nothing *obviously* wrong with the car—it drove smoothly and everything was just as it should be, especially for that price point. But from the moment I sat in the car to when we got back from the test drive, I could feel *something*. I don't know what it was... There was this weird buzzing sound in my ear. I felt uneasy, and no matter what I tried, I couldn't shake off that feeling. I know all this sounds stupid and strange, but there was something peculiar about that car.' He shrugged, and with a tight smile said, 'Call me crazy now?'

Rupa reached out and held her husband's hand. 'You know I will never think that you're crazy. It's definitely odd...whatever it is you felt...but if you're telling me there's something off about the car, I'm going to believe you.'

'Without any proof?'

'Yes.' She smiled. 'Because you are the most rational, sensible and logical man I know. And if you say there's something wrong, there must be something wrong. Also, because I love you.'

'I'm too lucky to have you,' he said, running his hand through her hair.

'So tell me...what exactly did you feel? Because you were sweating buckets. For a minute, I almost panicked thinking that you were having a heart attack...'

Amit went on to tell his wife in detail what he had felt that morning.

'Rupa, can you hear me?' Amit shouted into the phone.

'Barely...' she replied. 'What's happened?'

It was rush hour on Camac Street and the traffic roared into the phone.

'The car's broken down. It happened right in the middle of the road. I'm waiting for the tow truck to arrive and take it away.'

'Oh God! What happened to the car?'

'It's just done its time, I guess,' Amit said.

'Yes, we really need to buy a new one.'

'I think I see the tow truck. I'll be late getting back home,' Amit said and hung up.

The next morning at breakfast, they were discussing potential cars they could look at when Amit said, 'You know what...I would like to look at the Voltaus model again. It was a good car. Great specifications.'

Rupa was silent for a minute before she said, 'But what about the...how you felt that day?'

'I've thought a lot about it. It just seems irrational to dismiss something based on some weird feeling, right? So I'm thinking...why don't we give it another shot? I'll take it for another test drive and see how I feel this time. What do you think?'

'Makes sense,' Rupa said.

'I'll go to the showroom this Saturday.'

'Ah, I won't be able to make it. I've got a client meeting in Bhowanipore. Why don't you go on your own and tell me about it later? I mean I've already seen the car.'

'All right.'

Amit was the first customer in the Voltaus showroom

that Saturday. His reasoning was that a drive in the morning, with a clear mind, would help. Rahul greeted him warmly. They had spoken on the phone the previous day and Amit had told him that he would like to give the car another shot.

'Ready to go for a drive, sir?' Rahul said.

'I've never been more ready' Amit said, with a smile.

He took the keys from Rahul and got into the driver's seat. He turned on the ignition, pressed the accelerator and slowly drove the car out of the showroom compound. Amit was feeling positive about the car. If all went well, he would buy it this very morning.

They hit the highway, which was even more deserted in the morning. Amit pressed down on the accelerator, feeling the engine's power. Just then, the buzzing sound returned. This time it was louder. He tried to focus on the road, but that feeling of unease returned. It gripped his heart, making it beat faster. He started to sweat. Amit could no longer focus on the road.

'Something is not right...' he tried to say the words, but they came out as a mere whisper.

'Sir?' Rahul asked.

'Something isn't right...' Amit tried to speak up, but he couldn't. Suddenly, his vision grew blurry and he struggled to maintain control of the car. An image flashed before his eyes.

Streams of blood oozed out of the dashboard, the AC vents and the speakers.

'What...'

'Sir, are you okay?'

The streams gained strength. The blood was now pouring out, forming a pool at their feet.

Amit began to shout, 'Stop! Stop this!'

The car swerved sharply towards the highway's dividers. Rahul lurched forward and grabbed the steering wheel. Amit collapsed into his seat. He covered his eyes, screaming for it to stop. Rahul gained control of the car and brought it to a stop by the roadside. 'God!' he said in frustration. 'What are you doing, sir? You could have killed us both.'

Amit got out of the car and stood on the side of the road. He bent forward, taking deep breaths of fresh air. The buzzing sound stopped, his vision cleared and his heartbeat returned to normal. When he was able to speak, he turned to Rahul. 'I'm sorry. I don't know what happened there. But there's something wrong with this car.'

'There's nothing wrong with it,' Rahul snapped, but then quickly changed his tone. 'Maybe you need to go home and get some rest. Let me drive you back to the showroom.'

'Thanks. I think I'll call for an Uber here,' Amit said. 'I'm sorry for…for what happened…and taking up your time.'

'Are you sure, sir?' Rahul said impatiently.

'Yes.'

'Okay.' With that, Rahul got into the car and sped off down the highway.

It took Amit thirty minutes to find an Uber, but he didn't mind the wait. Anything was better than the nightmare of getting back into the Voltaus 203.

The incident gripped Amit like a fever. He couldn't stop thinking about it. Rupa told him to forget about it because it just didn't make any sense. Or, she had said, 'You could speak to my therapist about it...'

Amit had shrugged off the suggestion. Questions about the two incidents gnawed at him. Most nights, he found that he couldn't sleep. He would silently get out of bed and go sit at his desk. He looked up reviews of the car, and went on to Reddit and other forums. He watched each and every video there was reviewing this model and all he found were good reviews. There was nothing to indicate that there was anything wrong with the car. There was certainly no one out there who had experienced something similar to what he had.

He then went on to the website and began to look minutely at the information displayed on it. Everything seemed innocuous. One night, as he sat studying the website, something struck him. The batteries of these electric cars were made by extracting a lot of lithium and he realized he didn't know much about the element or how it worked in cars. He googled lithium and read this on Wikipedia:

'It is a soft, silvery-white alkali metal. Under standard conditions, it is the least dense metal and the least dense solid element. Like all alkali metals, lithium is highly reactive and flammable, and must be stored in a vacuum, inert atmosphere, or inert liquid such as purified kerosene or mineral oil. It exhibits a metallic lustre. It corrodes quickly in air to a dull silvery grey, then black tarnish. It does not occur freely in nature, but occurs mainly as pegmatitic minerals, which were once the main source of lithium.'

Amit began to scroll and found that there seemed to be a demand for lithium to make batteries for electric cars. As he read on, he found that lithium is mined in many geographically sensitive areas like Nevada, Chile and other parts of the world. The people who were native to these areas were also protesting against these lithium mines. So, although these electric cars were marketed and manufactured as the future of vehicles with reduced carbon emissions, thanks to their use of renewable energy sources, there was a murkier truth behind them—the fact that using lithium wasn't such an ecological solution as initially believed.

But underneath all this was an even larger problem—one that was rarely mentioned by anyone. Most lithium mines employed unregulated child labour. In South America, there is the 'Lithium Triangle', a region of the Andes, which covers parts of Chile, Argentina and Bolivia. In Africa, the Democratic Republic of the Congo struggled with this issue, as did parts of China. More than one million children are employed in the mining industry, which is a hazardous industry. They are employed in the extraction and transportation of these chemicals, often handling these toxic substances with their bare hands. Mines are not ventilated, so most of these children suffer respiratory diseases and many also die on the job.

Amit was shocked by the data. He had never known that the batteries of new smartphones and 'environmentally safe' electric cars had so much blood on their hands. How much would we pay in the quest for new, cutting-edge technologies? he thought.

Now, he understood his visions. The blood he had seen in the car was the blood of these children—young, innocent and enslaved by a despotic and brutal system.

He shut his laptop and stood up, making his way to the balcony. He considered their society. How green was Green Views actually? He needed to be more careful about their choices, or what earth were they going to leave behind for the coming generations?

As he sat on his balcony, the wind silent for a change, Amit looked up at the sky, at the stars playing hide-and-seek from behind the clouds and prayed. But even as he did, he knew deep down that nothing would come of his prayers. The world was too far gone and there was nothing we could do that would pull it back from the fires of hell.

6

The Great Beauty

Urmila walked out of her house to the gate and opened the small flap on the mailbox, pulling out the envelopes that were sitting there. Before heading back into the house, she took a moment to absorb her surroundings. Winter was almost over, and the morning sunlight had a wonderful warmth in it that thawed her icy bones. Taking a deep breath, she felt the clean mountain air fill her lungs, smelling of pine and herbs. Around her small garden patch, tiny spring flowers were bursting out of the cold earth, while a flock of yellow butterflies floated around the freshly dug flower beds that housed petunias, chrysanthemums and snapdragons. She pulled her shawl tightly around herself as she admired the beauty of the small cottage her father had left to her in his will when he had died five years ago.

Urmila barely remembered her mother; she was only five years old when her mother lost her battle with cancer. It was her father who had raised and cared for her, teaching her the ways of the world and how to survive in it. He had been not only her father but also her friend, mentor and spiritual guide. So when he died suddenly in the dead of night, succumbing to a heart attack, Urmila not only lost her last living parent but also her best friend. On this crisp and bright morning, she missed him dearly. This little red brick house and garden were all that she had in the world, but as she started walking back to the house, clutching the envelopes tightly in her hand, she hoped that today things would change slightly.

Inside, Urmila made her way to the small round dining table, pulling out a chair to sit down. She took a sip of her now cold tea as she flipped through her mail. Most of them were simply subscriptions and advertisements from local companies, but when she saw a government stamp on one of the envelopes, she stopped and pulled it out of the pile. Her heart beat faster. Urmila had been waiting for this letter for over six months. She quickly ripped open the envelope, pulled out the letter and started reading it. Urmila smiled as her gaze quickly moved over the lines confirming that she indeed was now a lessor of the surrounding one acre of land near her home. What had started out as a whim had now become a reality and this realization made her extremely happy.

'Only time will make things better,' a well-meaning friend had told Urmila on that fateful day when judgment had been pronounced on her.

Urmila was an assistant manager at the Glenbrook Tea

Estate in Darjeeling. She had been in the position for five years and was due for a promotion. A week before the yearly appraisals, there had been a dinner party at the general manager of the estate, her boss's bungalow. The party began as all tea garden parties do, with a lot of alcohol and snacks. Urmila, a teetotaller, found this tradition of heavy drinking, which was rampant in tea garden culture, very bothersome. Perhaps it was the lack of entertainment or the isolation of tea gardens from towns and other activities, but alcohol played a prominent role in the lives of most tea estate employees.

That evening, Urmila stuck to her soda and socialized among her peers, bosses and other guests who had driven many kilometres to attend. Since it was her boss's party, it was customary for junior employees to stay until the very end, ensuring that the guests had their dinner and drink refills and were seen safely back to their cars as they left. It was late when Urmila grabbed her bag and approached her boss to bid him goodnight. However, her boss seemed to have other ideas. He asked Urmila to join him in the guest room to look at something and she agreed. Urmila didn't think too much of it because her boss was a married man and his two children were away at boarding school.

In the guest room, however, Urmila felt a wave of unease when her boss asked her to sit beside him on the lounge chair. He seemed to ramble away about nothing in particular, and when she enquired about what he wanted to show her, he placed his hand on her thigh and leaned over to kiss her. Urmila jumped up in shock, the blood draining from her face. Before she could react, he grabbed her hand, pulling her down so that she fell into his lap. He held her tightly and continued trying to kiss her as he groped her body. Urmila pushed against him with all her might, but it was only when she kicked his shin with the heel of her boot that he cried out in pain and released her. Without hesitation, Urmila ran out of the room, down the veranda steps, and towards where her car was parked. She got in and drove straight home, her mind filled with a thousand thoughts.

That night, Urmila could not sleep. She tossed and turned in her bed, then rose and paced her room until she was exhausted. She was conflicted about what she should do. Her boss had sexually assaulted her, yet she couldn't help but think of all the years of hard work she had put into her role and the fact that she was finally up for a promotion and a significant raise. However, would money absolve her of the guilt if she did not speak about what had happened to her? If she did not report the incident to the authorities, who knows how many other young women her boss would assault in the coming years. The mere thought made her feel sick to the stomach. As the night faded into dawn and the sound of birds filled the early morning skies, Urmila came to a decision. She knew what she had to do. Immediately, she went to her desk, booted up her laptop and wrote a firm and honest email to the company's board, hoping they would lend her their ear and deliver a just decision.

Urmila did not hear back from the company's board until a week later. She was a nervous wreck. Not only was she worried about the consequences of the email, but she also had to spend many uncomfortable hours working with her boss in the office. However, her boss pretended as though nothing had happened that night.

On the following Saturday, at the end of their working week, she received an email from her boss asking her to meet him after lunch in his office as he had something he wanted to discuss with her. When Urmila made her way to his office that afternoon, she found that they were not alone; they had been joined by a representative of the company's board. In the hour that followed, Urmila felt sick, humiliated and violated in every possible way because, as it transpired, the board had decided that Urmila's accusation against her boss was baseless and that she had no proof to support her grievous claims. Her boss also seemed to insinuate that she was too ambitious for her own good and her actual intention was to get rid of him because he was a threat to her professionally, and in doing so, she would benefit in her career. The board had come to the conclusion that Urmila needed to leave the company as soon as possible. They gave her severance, but they wanted her to vacate her premises and leave the garden within a week. On her way back to her bungalow, Urmila laughed, thinking about how her hard work, perseverance and honesty had paid her.

And that was how Urmila found herself back in the small cottage that her father had left to her on the outskirts of Darjeeling, on a quiet hill full of pine and juniper trees. In the months that followed, Urmila did a bit of freelancing so that she had some income flowing in every month, but more and more, she found herself drawn to the garden that surrounded her small home. Every day, she woke up early, had a cup of tea and a quick bite, and then put on her garden boots and went outside. She was amazed by how much work a garden demanded. There were the daily tasks of pruning and removing leaf litter; she began to learn the magic of composting and how it could be used back in the garden as a rich fertilizer. As summer turned to autumn and then to winter, her gardening chores changed with every season. In summer, she needed to protect her plants from the severe heat and sow seeds for the next season; in autumn, there was the profusion of leaf litter that she turned into compost, and in winter, there was not much she could do as she watched the ground turn into solid ice, only being able to bring a few of her potted plants inside the house to shelter them from the brutal cold.

Every night, before she went to bed, she made it a habit to study botany and read up about planting and gardening and the terrain she was dealing with. She went to the local library and found books about native plants, shrubs and trees and studied these books deeply. Besides reading, she found the task of gardening extremely meditative, humbling and very rewarding. As the days went by, a small dream began to form in her mind. She imagined leasing a larger plot of land where she could grow native medicinal plants and trees that would not only benefit people but also give back to the region. The plot of land could also become a suitable example of permaculture.

The more she read about horticulture, the more she began

to understand and realize the destructive aspect of agriculture. Agriculture primarily focused on growing a single type of crop repeatedly, gradually depleting the land of its nutrients and minerals. Permaculture, on the other hand, was a system of horticulture in which many different symbiotic crops were grown at the same time and each crop benefited the other, while also enriching the soil it grew in. She was convinced this was the only way forward and that the future would be all about permaculture.

But this was all still a dream until one day, Urmila stumbled across a website detailing the process of how she could rent a plot of land from the government to carry out this little project. She read through the details and the fine print, then filled out the form and paid the necessary fees to make this happen. With her fingers crossed, she submitted all her documents, and then the long wait for approval or rejection began.

So this was why Urmila was over the moon to find that her application to lease the land from the government had been approved. The plot, in particular, was just a ten-minute walk away from Urmila's home. She put down the letter, finished her cup of tea, and went upstairs to change into a thick jacket and a warm pair of trousers. Once done, she put on her walking boots and headed out in the direction of the plot of land of which she now was the landlady. Excitement surged through her entire being as she thought of how she could transform this small plot of land into what she had been dreaming of all these days.

Ten minutes later, she was standing at the site, observing every square foot of the barren patch of land which had only a few overgrown shrubs and a lot of weeds choking its surface. She knew it was going to be backbreaking work to clear out this space, till the land and add fertilizers and nutrients back into the soil so that it became a fertile patch of land ready for planting. Urmila was prepared for the hard work, but it would make her life a tad bit easier if she had just one pair of extra hands to help her with the daily tasks. An idea suddenly took root in her mind. She thought back to Asha, a widow who had worked in Urmila's bungalow as a washerwoman and had also helped with the daily errands. Urmila was not one to wait. She pulled out her phone from her jacket pocket and dialled Asha's number. When Asha picked up, Urmila ran her through her idea and told her about the job that she was offering. Asha heard Urmila out and immediately accepted it because she wanted to get away from the tea gardens in which she saw no future for herself. So just like that, Urmila's little dream had developed wings.

It took Urmila and Asha a whole month just to clear out the patch of land and fertilize it. Obviously, they had to work during daylight hours only, and since Urmila also had to do her freelance work to earn money, time was short. But as spring turned into summer and the days grew longer, the two women found more time to be outside and work the land. A month later, the land was ready for planting. Urmila had planned out a whole list of complementary plants that could be sown together.

One day, the two women drove down to the local nursery and bought many packets of seeds, manure, natural insect repellents, watering pipes and other accessories they required for the summer months. Together, they planted lavender, tomatoes, beans, citronella, sage, local varieties of medicinal herbs and some forms of smaller fruit trees native to the region. Under the sweltering sun, with their backs bent, the two women found a steady rhythm of working, chatting and problem-solving. At the end of the day, when they went back to the cottage, the women were exhausted but they also felt like they had achieved something. Urmila offered Asha the guest room in her house so that she did not have to live somewhere far away and spend her salary on rent and travel.

As the days passed, they developed a friendship that was akin to family. They worked together, made their meals together and ate together, discussing both the seriousness and frivolousness of life, but most importantly, always talking about the piece of land that they tended to with their whole hearts. Urmila became more and more convinced that the idea of leasing this plot of land was the best decision she had made in her life as she watched the seeds they had planted sprout into tiny saplings and then grow into sturdy plants.

Of course they had their challenges. Many times, their fledgling garden was attacked by insects, fungi or other diseases. Then there was a storm that nearly flattened their garden. In the peak of summer, they had to cover the entire space with shade cloths so that the young plants did not wither away. There was always something that needed to be done; there was always a problem that needed solving. But, at the end of the day, the result was always more satisfying than anything Urmila had ever imagined, especially when their plants grew big and strong, started producing flowers and slowly bore fruit.

Soon, most of the vegetables and herbs they used in the kitchen came directly from their garden. In fact, sometimes they had more than they could consume, so Urmila or Asha would go down to the local market and sell the excess produce. This produce soon grew in demand because the fruits and vegetables were grown using organic methods, thus tasting sweeter and juicier than most of the produce available in the market. Urmila had to constantly tell the shopkeepers to whom she sold her produce that she could not provide more than a certain amount because she did not have the capacity, as she had only a small plot of land. Basically, she explained to them that she was actually just getting rid of the excess produce so that it would not rot and go to waste.

One day, an unexpected visitor arrived at Urmila's doorstep. It was a man who introduced himself as Vinay.

'Hello ma'am,' Vinay said, handing Urmila his card. 'I'm from Greenhouse Economics and I happened to be in a shop in town where the shopkeeper could not stop talking about the wonderful produce you are selling to him. So I did a bit of research and I understand that you have a registered plantation?'

They were still standing at the gate.

'It's hardly a plantation.' Urmila laughed. 'It's actually

just a small garden...well...not really small but enough to keep my kitchen going and a little more. But yes, I have registered it.'

'That's wonderful,' said Vinay. 'Actually, that is why I have come here, to talk to you about your garden.'

'Sure,' opening the gate, she said, 'why don't you come inside and we can have a cup of tea and talk further.'

'Okay, that would be nice,' Vinay said. 'Thank you.'

Urmila showed Vinay to her dining table while she made them a pot of tea. Once the tea was ready, she brought the teapot, two cups, a small pot of milk and sugar to the table. She poured them both some tea and then sat down.

'So, what is it that you want to talk to me about?' Urmila asked.

'It's actually very simple...' Vinay said. 'I wanted to know if you would be interested in selling your carbon credits. You see... the company I work at specializes in green technology and carbon credits. We provide a carbon credit platform known as Green Marketplace.'

Urmila smiled. 'Well... Vinay... First, you would need to tell me more about carbon credits because, to be very honest, I am absolutely at sea here.'

Vinay took a sip of his tea and then spoke. 'Okay, I'll try and explain it to you. You have a plantation, and this plantation, because it is filled with trees and vegetation, begins to act like a sponge for carbon dioxide from the atmosphere over time. As you must know, plants absorb carbon dioxide and convert it into energy. That is their primary energy source and that is how plants live and thrive. Does this make sense till now?'

'Yes,' Urmila said. 'Carry on.'

'So, over time, your plantation acts like a carbon sink. Two examples of the biggest carbon sinks on earth are forests and oceans. Now, we come to carbon credits. Carbon credits are measurable, verifiable emission reductions from certified climate action projects. These projects reduce, remove or avoid greenhouse gas emissions. They also bring a whole host of other positive benefits, for example, they empower communities, protect ecosystems, restore forests or reduce reliance on fossil fuels.'

'Yes,' Urmila said. 'But how does this affect me?'

'Well… you could go online and check how many carbon credits your plantation has accumulated and you could choose to sell them for a neat profit.'

'Ah… okay,' she said. 'But who do I sell them to?'

'Companies like mine,' Vinay said.

'Okay, now all of this makes sense,' Urmila said.

They had finished their tea, and Vinay said, 'No pressure. Here's my card. I know you need time to think about it and also do your research but if you ever feel like you've come to a decision and you would like to sell your credits, do give me a call.'

'Thanks so much, Vinay,' she said. 'You've introduced me to a whole new world that I had no clue about.' She smiled.

'I better get going. Thank you so much for the tea and for hearing me out,' Vinay said.

'No problem. The pleasure is mine,' she said.

They stood up, and Urmila showed Vinay to the gate and waved him goodbye. Five minutes later, she was at her desk, on her laptop, googling carbon credits and carbon sinks. Although she had known nothing about these subjects, she was curious by what the man had told her. She had no idea that her small patch of land could accrue benefits of this scale. She wanted to know more about how carbon credits worked and if there was something meaningful she could do with them. That night, Urmila stayed up late reading about the subject. She came across a website that could quantify the number of credits any plantation owner had accumulated over a period of time. And she was shocked to find out that her garden had accumulated a number of these carbon credits.

Urmila continued her research on the subject, and a week later, on one of the websites she was browsing, she came across the name of an IAS officer who had given a lecture on the subject at a college in the neighbouring city. She dug deep and found his contact details and quickly shot him an email, asking if they could get on a call in the near future as she had watched his lecture and wanted to discuss the prospect of carbon credits with him in detail. Two days later, the IAS officer, Mr Sharma, replied. He gave her a time to call him later that afternoon.

Sharp at 3 p.m., Urmila rang Mr Sharma. She knew that IAS officers were busy people, so she got to the point. She told him about Vinay's visit and what he had told her about her small plantation accumulating carbon credits. She also told him that Vinay wanted her to sell these credits to his company. She asked Mr Sharma for his advice and what she should be doing in the near future.

Mr Sharma took some time to think over what she had said. He asked her a few details—like the size of her plantation, how long she had been tending to it, what kind of energy it consumed and whether she would be able to expand her plantation in the coming years.

'Look,' Mr Sharma said, 'carbon credits are a relatively new market entry and not many people in India are using them or even talking about them. But don't let that dissuade you because it is happening. Green and clean energy is the future. However, from what I understand, your garden, as you call it, is pretty small, although you say that you have calculated the amount of carbon credits it has accumulated. Most of the projects associated with carbon credits are usually quite largescale but that doesn't mean anything really. See, to be very honest, this is not my speciality, even though I am very interested in the subject. However, there is someone I know in the central government who I can connect you to and you could discuss it further with them.'

'All right, thank you so much for your time, sir. This has really helped me. I will think about it in more detail and consider what my options are for the future. But if you could connect me to your contact in the central government, that would be a big help for me,' she said.

'Not a problem,' Mr Sharma said. 'I will email you the details.'

'Any advice before you go?' Urmila asked.

'Well... the only thing I can think of is to keep the information about how many credits you have to yourself! It's a new market... and it's always wise to keep new ideas under a lid until they're solidified,' Mr Sharma said with a laugh and then they hung up.

Urmila's imagination had once again been fired. Her entrepreneurial spirit and can-do attitude kept her up on most nights as she strategized and planned her future. Finally she came to a decision. She realized that if she were to accumulate enough carbon credits, then that would mean something. She needed to expand her so-called garden into a proper plantation. In the following weeks, Urmila once again set about scouring the region, looking for a bigger plot of land. Upon finding it, she completed the paperwork again for its registration and lease. She knew the waiting period would be excruciating for her, so she threw herself into work and also into solidifying the plans for this larger plantation. Urmila had not stopped doing her freelance work as it brought home money. During this time, she also set up a small office space consisting of just two rooms within the garden on her compound. She also hired two young individuals and trained them for the work that would keep them busy once the registration was approved.

During this period, she found out about a Green Conference taking place in Delhi in a few months. She registered herself and her two employees for it, and when the time came, they flew to Delhi and attended the three-day conference. The Green Conference was a window to a new world. Urmila felt like she had just been scratching the surface of this new subject so far, and in those three days alone she had gained a much better understanding of it. Not only that, but the conference also gave her the opportunity to meet many people in the community. She met manufacturers, sellers, people who traded in carbon credits, journalists, investors and many others.

Back home, Urmila knew what she had to do. She set up a company and registered it, calling it Green Vistas. In essence, the goal of Green Vistas was to trade in the carbon credit market. By this time, approval for the bigger piece of land had also come through. This time, she gave Asha the responsibility of hiring more people and overseeing the cultivation of the land. Urmila had also contacted and discussed a better permaculture plan with a few environmentalists and horticulturalists. She aimed to implement slight changes so that the second plantation yielded a higher value of carbon credits.

Urmila had never imagined the scale of success awaiting her. As it turned out, carbon credits were in high demand among manufacturing and automobile companies striving to reach net zero in carbon emissions. Green Vistas became one of the first legitimate companies in this sector, and thus the demand for carbon credits grew exponentially. In less than a year, Green Vistas became a highly valued company known for its integrity and efficient, professional models. Urmila became a market leader in her segment. She received many offers from international companies, with offers to sell her own company or to join big multinationals in very senior positions. Turning down these offers was not easy, but Urmila was determined to give back to the place where she had grown up and the place that had nurtured her success. So she chose to stay back in Darjeeling. During this time, she grew her company and employed many more people, most of whom were women. Her fame grew across the region. Every other day, journalists were at her office interviewing her or taking photos of her for their magazines and newspapers. She was perceived as a woman who, through sheer hard work and an entrepreneurial spirit, had risen to the top yet chose to stick to her humble roots.

Urmila also received offers to purchase tea estates, and this was something that caught her fancy. She decided to acquire one such tea garden, not only because it would further her goals on carbon credits but also because a glimmer of a plan emerged in her mind. When she was signing the papers for the acquisition of the tea garden, she promised herself that she would be making some big changes not only in the estate that she had acquired but, if possible, in how tea gardens functioned across the region. One of the issues that was very close to her heart was equal pay for women and ensuring their safety from bullying and sexual predators in the workspace. To achieve this end, she hired one of West Bengal's best lawyers and set about fighting a case with the Indian Tea Association on how these changes could be implemented. She received immense pressure, threats to her life and many other challenges from the tea association board because they were rooted in very masculine and traditionalist cultures.

One Sunday evening, Asha and Urmila sat on the porch of her house. Urmila had not given up the small cottage that her father had left to her, and Asha had continued to live with her. They had been together for many years now, through all of life's ups and downs, and had become best friends. Urmila trusted Asha with her life. She could not imagine her success without Asha being her foundation.

It was November. The season was turning again. Winter was in the air and the stars were sparkling brightly in the sky. Asha was reading out a newspaper article in Bengali about Urmila.

'She is the uncontested leader of carbon credits in North-Eastern India. She is a success story with soul.' Asha finished reading and put the newspaper aside. 'What a long way you have come, my dear,' she said.

Urmila looked up at the clear sky. 'We,' she said softly, 'what a long way we have come.'

'Yes,' Asha said.

They were silent for a moment before Urmila spoke. 'And we still have a long way to go.'

'Of course,' Asha said. 'But for now…enjoy this moment. The road ahead seems endless, but it will come to an end one day. You will want to look back at these moments and be grateful that you took a moment to appreciate this great beauty.'

In the distance, the pines stood like giant soldiers against the dusk. Fireflies twinkled in the grass. The moon lit up the last of the white flowers in the garden.

'Yes,' Urmila said, taking a deep breath. 'We are nothing without this great beauty.'

Carbon credit is the most upcoming industry in the environmental and climate crisis management area. Creating awareness and making the planet a better place to live in is the main goal of this short story.

7

The Language of Painting

As usual, the queue for the public toilet is very long. At least fifteen people stand in line, holding on to mugs and bars of soap, waiting for their turn. In the blistering summer heat, the people soon grow irritable, and the children start crying while the mothers grow weary. It is not even 7 a.m. and life in the Rajabagan slum in west Kolkata feels like one continuous wait.

Mini can do nothing but wait until she reaches the front of the queue. The simple act of accessing a private loo is a luxury here. Yet, even this misery seems preferable to Mini because, like the others in front and behind her who all live in this sprawling slum, she doesn't have a home to call her own. At night, she divides her time seeking shelter in three different houses, rotating among them each night, thanks to the good grace of these families who have welcomed her despite their cramped quarters.

Mini is one of the millions of homeless people in Kolkata. Every day is a struggle. She wakes up, joins the queue for one of the public toilets in the slum, cleans herself, then hits the streets—where she eats, walks, works—until the day ends and she returns to the slum to rest her weary body on the hard floor of someone's small home. It wasn't always like this for Mini, but that is a story for another time.

Though homeless, Mini doesn't beg; she is far too proud for that. Every day, she finds odd jobs to buy her meals and saves every rupee she doesn't spend on food. When she has nothing to do, she returns to an abandoned playground tucked between a market and a fabric factory. It is here that she spends most of her time when she isn't working. Mini has a secret—one that keeps her alive.

It is her passion for creating art. Just as tigers are born to hunt or a caterpillar is destined to transform into a cocoon and then a butterfly, or how birds fly south in the winter months, Mini has always painted. It comes naturally to her, like a primal instinct she cannot control. Even now, with no money to buy paper or pens, Mini uses fallen twigs and stones to create artwork on the earth of the playground.

The people in the market soon catch on to Mini's 'talent' and they think her a madwoman, indulging her with some scrap paper and ink. She uses every 'donation' judiciously, contemplating deeply about what she will create before putting ink to paper. At the end of the day, she usually reciprocates these favours by presenting the 'donors' with a gift of her art. Her paintings are beautiful; she brings to life landscapes so ethereal they transport the viewer deep into their imaginations. Her dreamscapes are vivid and alluring, while she also creates charming depictions of trees and birds for children. Everyone is mesmerized by the beauty of these works of art.

One day, a woman who works at the fabric factory spots these artworks and gifts Mini a whole bale of cut-up cloth— essentially scraps. 'Perhaps this may be of some use to you. It's all I can do,' she says to Mini. To others, this bundle of scrap material could simply be junk to be tossed away, but to Mini, it is a goldmine. She asks the woman for a needle and some thread, and when supplied with them, she spends all her free time—staying up at night under the light of the slum's street light—sewing together every little scrap material to create a five-metre-long sheet of cloth. After a long time she feels alive, as though there is purpose in her life, and it liberates her from the daily fatigue of a long, frustrating day out on the streets with nothing to call her own.

When she is finally done, Mini has in her possession a canvas longer and larger than any 'space' she has had to create her art. She already has a sense of what she wants to draw on it: a lifelike image of a slice of her life in the slums. She wants to paint it in all its filth and squalor but also highlight the little joys and the sense of community she witnesses each day. But where will she get the paints to bring this artwork to life?

Mini begins to scrutinize her surroundings with an eagle's eye. Then it strikes her. The answer has been in front of her all along. All she needs to do is be creative and entrepreneurial. So in the following days, Mini turns into a scavenger—a scavenger of natural paint materials. She visits the huge and sprawling *sabzi mandis* and picks up turmeric pods and banana flowers that are being thrown away. She collects hibiscus flowers and jamun fruits that fall from the trees strewn across the city. There are certain leaves that produce a bright green pigment and marigolds for their orange hue. One shopkeeper gives her a box of *sindoor* that has broken, and another a piece of *kajal* pencil. When she has collected enough 'paints' for her piece, Mini starts to work. She works tirelessly in the hours when she isn't doing her daily wage labour jobs, first sketching out her scene which she has already imagined in vivid detail. She knows her entire painting as intimately as the lines of her palms because, in her mind's eye, she must—she does not have the luxury of a do-over. She uses the kajal pencil to sketch out her piece, then begins to paint it in. In a week, she has created the most wondrous piece of artwork anyone in the vicinity had ever chanced upon. The slumdwellers come to look at it; the ones who have phones, which many do, take photos and put them up on their Facebook accounts. Her painting goes viral, and soon, a few folks offer her more donations of actual paper and paints.

Mini feels blessed with these gifts. She begins to paint in traditional Bengali techniques, her favourite being 'pattachitra'. Meanwhile, a few mothers from the slum approach Mini, asking her if she will teach their children how to paint—it is a better use of their time than wandering the city aimlessly.

So, every Sunday, Mini starts a small class under the slum's only banyan tree. At first, there are just a few students, five in total. But soon, the class begins to grow, and six months later, Mini is teaching at least twenty young children from the slum a weekly art class for which she gets paid a few rupees each from every parent. This money means a lot to Mini. She is finally able to rent a small quarter in the slum for herself. It is not home, but it is her very own place where she can come back after the daily toil and rest her head on her own pillow. The feeling is magical. Mini is determined to teach her students better and also work on pieces that inspire the people who view them.

One day, Mini reads about an exciting event happening in Murshidabad, a city over 200 kilometres away from Kolkata, in the local newspaper. It is an open call to artists to submit their portfolio of work to be included among other more established artists in an exhibition. The terms and conditions are simple: a small fee and anyone—no bars on age or gender or qualifications—can apply. This call seems to be a sign from heaven. Mini tears up the advertisement and goes home, her heart beating fiercely in her chest.

Back in her small room, she counts out her savings and realizes she has just enough to make the journey to Murshidabad and also create a portfolio of all her paintings. The application for the exhibition is two weeks away and

Mini decides she can paint a few more works before she has to make her submission.

Mini works like a woman possessed. She barely eats or sleeps; she does the bare minimum of her daily wage jobs, spending all the time she can creating her best pieces. Yet she does not feel fatigued, for her soul has been awakened and she knows she is doing what she is destined to do. It is a call from the heavens itself and Mini feels that she is fulfilling her destiny.

Two weeks pass by in the blink of an eye, and after making the journey to Murshidabad to submit her portfolio and application, Mini returns to Kolkata. She goes about her days but cannot stop thinking about her submission. What if her application is rejected? What if she simply isn't good enough? After all, she is just an amateur who is working with the simplest materials. Of course, there are others who have access to better paints, brushes, canvases and paper, all of which will result in superior works of art. The very thought makes her feel dejected momentarily, but there is nothing she can do to control the outcome. She has done her best; the rest is up to Goddess Durga.

A month later, the results of the competition are declared in the same local newspaper. But two days before that, on a sweltering morning, her neighbour comes rushing into her room.

'Mini, Mini…' the woman says. 'A call for you from Murshidabad. Something about a competition.'

Mini jumps up from her cot and grabs the phone, her long

loose hair undone from its bun. She listens carefully to what the speaker, an administrative person from the art institute, is saying. When she realizes what the man is saying, her heart explodes with happiness. She has won the competition! Her works are going to be displayed among those of well-known artists of the time. Mini listens to all the instructions the man is giving her: she has to travel to Murshidabad, although this time her travel expenses would be paid, bringing with her all her original pieces but with their frames, which would also be paid for. She would have to give a few press interviews about her work and her experience regarding the competition. Mini complies with all the man's instructions.

Later, after she has hung up and returned the phone to her neighbour, Mini takes a few moments to sit down and say a soft prayer to Goddess Durga, the one who has stood by her during her times of strife, the one who gives her the courage to face each day, the one who has seeded this talent in her, guided her and finally blessed her with this bounty. Without the Goddess, she would have been lost. Little did Mini know that this win was going to change her life forever.

A year later, Mini sits in a relatively empty teacher's common room, sipping her cup of tea. She gazes out of the windows at the manicured lawns, watching the trees shed their leaves in the wind. It is fall and already there is the sense of festivity in the air. Not for the first time, Mini offers a little prayer, thanking her destiny for where it has brought her.

After the competition in Murshidabad and subsequent press interviews, which were enormously successful, Mini started receiving more and more opportunities to exhibit her works across West Bengal. Her work appealed to everyone who viewed it because it was rooted in honesty and beauty. The word about this self-taught artist from the slums also made for a great cover story and Mini was featured in many well-known magazines and journals from the state. All these things helped Mini consolidate her reputation as an artist so that when the scholarship for an assistant art professor at Calcutta University was advertised and Mini applied, the board was only too happy to award it to this rising star. So this is how Mini secured one of the most coveted teaching positions at this prestigious university.

That day, after she finishes her classes, Mini gathers the art materials, closes the big, echoing art hall and packs her bag. She has rented a small flat just a thirty-minute walk away from the university campus. On most days, Mini prefers to walk home. She loves to take in the sights and sounds of her beloved city—the yellow cabs honking at each other, the crowds gathering next to the *puchka wallah* in the evening near one of the university gates, which is thronged by students and others for a delicious evening snack. The scent of parijat flowers suffuses the air and she can sense Pujo approaching.

She walks slowly, revelling in these details that make up life—the aspects and nuances that she captures on paper and brings to life with paint. It is a time of reflection and meditation. So, unless it is raining very heavily or she is feeling unwell, Mini always takes this time to walk back home.

Her flat is tucked away in a quiet street, behind an otherwise bustling market. Most of the buildings here are rented out to students or journalists. The rents are on the lower side because the flats are of older construction. Mini doesn't mind that they are sometimes quite decrepit. These older constructions have higher ceilings and airy rooms that are larger than newer buildings with sleeker fittings and amenities. She loves the rough, old stone steps and the cool, dark corridors. As she makes her way up these stairs, her mind filled with the day's activities, she senses something that makes her stop.

Her hair stands on end at the back of her neck and her blood runs cold. Something is wrong and she can sense it like an animal threatened. She makes her way up the last few steps to her floor, and at the end of the hallway, she spots a familiar figure leaning against the wall in front of her door, the glow on his phone illuminating his face.

He has returned.

The man senses her presence and looks up from his phone at Mini.

'I thought you'd never come back. How long I've been waiting for you...' his voice trails off lazily.

'Alok?' Mini barely manages the word. She feels a sinking

feeling in her stomach. 'What are you doing here?'

'Like I said…waiting for you,' the man says. He straightens up and begins to slowly walk towards her.

Mini wants to run but she is frozen to the spot.

'Don't look so scared.' The man laughs. 'I won't bite you.'

He walks to where she is standing, and when he is at arm's length from her, he reaches out to take her bag. 'Why don't you give me that…it looks heavy…'

Mini's soul leaves her body. She feels the bag slide from her hand and into his grasp. She cannot speak or move. She has turned to stone.

'Come, you look like you've had a long day…' he says. 'Why don't you let us in, and I'll make us both a cup of tea…'

Mini wants to shout for help and flee; instead, she feels her body move automatically to his suggestion. The many years of his control had programmed her like a computer. Mini moves like a zombie. She opens the door to her flat and flicks on the lights after stepping inside.

Alok follows her in. The flat comprises a one-bedroom space with a small hall, a kitchen and a bathroom. The hall opens out on to a big balcony that overlooks the street.

'Neat place you've got here,' Alok says, dropping Mini's bag to the floor, which falls with a loud thud. 'Small, so it makes things easier to find.'

'How did you find me?' Mini finally speaks. The condescension in his voice has made her snap out of her fear. She feels anger bubble up inside her like a volcano ready to erupt. How dare he mock my home, she thinks.

'That was very easy,' Alok says with a smile as he makes his way to the kitchen, opening and slamming cupboards. He finds a pan, the tea and sugar, and then starts boiling some water. 'Now where do you keep your cups…. ah found them.'

'How did you find me, I asked?'

'You're quite famous, Miss Artist from the slums,' Alok says, banging down two cups on the kitchen counter. It is a wonder they don't break. 'I've been following your journey for quite some time. And once you joined the university as an assistant art professor, it was just a matter of looking for you and following you home. Simple.'

Mini keeps silent.

'In fact,' Alok says with a laugh, 'I find it funny how it was you yourself who helped me find you after you abandoned me. Crazy how these things work, right?'

Abandoned—the word strikes Mini in her gut. She feels like she has been punched, and the wind leaves her body with a force so strong it takes the ground from underneath her feet.

'I didn't abandon you, Alok,' Mini says through gritted teeth. 'I ran away because you were…you were…'

'I was what?' Alok snaps at her. The water boils and he throws two teabags into the cups and splashes hot water over them.

She doesn't reply. 'What happened to Miss Famous Artist always giving interviews—cat got your tongue?' He brings the tea to her and puts it down on the small table beside her.

'You used to hit me, Alok,' Mini says softly. 'A lot.'

Alok snorts. 'Hit you…' he sneers. 'A husband has some rights over his woman. And every marriage has ups and downs. Just because I hit you once or twice doesn't mean that you abandon your husband whom you had vowed to stick by through sickness and health.'

'You put me in the hospital twice,' Mini says softly. 'Five broken ribs, a broken nose, fractured shin and arms. You disfigured my face.'

Alok sits down on the chair in the hall and looks at the ceiling. 'You still haven't learnt to say thank you.'

'For what?' Mini says.

'The tea that I made for you…' Alok says, with a nod at the cup that he set beside her.

'I have nothing to thank you for,' Mini says. 'My life was a living hell with you, and then I chose to leave, or I would not have lived to see this day. I spent every day out on the streets. I lived in the slums, and was homeless for years. Do you know what that's like? Or how hard it can be out there? Do you know how it can break someone? Especially someone who grew up with loving parents in a secure home?'

'Don't lecture me, Mini.' He turns to her with a fierceness in his eyes that sends a chill down her spine. 'All I know is that my *wife* ran away and left me to deal with everything on my own. All the gossip and rumours. Did you even think for a moment how I survived on my own? Huh? Of course, you didn't, you selfish ghoul. You only think about yourself and your sob story. Well, now I've come to take back what's mine.'

Mini wants to scream. Scream till her voice turns hoarse. She feels the panic, the desperation, the anger, the fear—all the old feelings rise in her simultaneously. For the ten years that she was married to Alok, this cocktail of emotions was what she felt every day when she was with him, and now that nightmare—the one she thought she had shaken off—was back in her living room like a ghost.

'I'm not going back with you,' she says firmly. A vein throbs in her forehead.

Alok looks at her, surprised. The fierce look in his eye disappears and his face breaks into a grin. Then, he bursts into laughter, loud and raucous. 'That's really funny!' he snorts. 'Why would you think I want you back? I haven't gone crazy. I mean just look at your face.'

'It's the face you made, Alok,' she says furiously. 'So, what the hell do you want from me now?'

Alok goes still. He turns to her and says calmly, 'I want a percentage of all sales from your work…for life…50 per cent to be exact.'

It takes a moment for the words to sink in. Mini clenches her fists tightly. 'How dare you? How dare you even ask for that! It's my whole life's work, why should I give you even a rupee of my hard earned money?'

'Because…my dear *wife*…' Alok says, stressing the word, 'we are still not divorced, and thus you are rightfully still my wife, and I am entitled to your income. Now, if we were to get a divorce, this is the only compensation I am asking.' He picks up his cup of tea, which has gone cold by now, and drinks all of it at once.

He rises, looks around her house and says, 'You've only just started your career. I know things will get better for you. You're very talented. So don't look so disheartened. You'll be rich one day. I just know it.'

Alok makes his way to the door. Before leaving, he turns to her and says, 'My lawyer will send you the papers.'

The door slams shut and Mini drops her face in her palms and bursts into tears. What a fool she is, she thinks, to believe she was free. What an utter fool!

Two weeks later, an envelope arrives at her flat's pigeonhole. Inside is a notarized letter from Alok's lawyer, containing a legal document stating that she had abandoned him when he was medically unwell and thus he is seeking a divorce with the terms and conditions for the way forward, including the damages that Mini must pay him.

Mini reads the notice many times before tossing it away. She thinks about hiring a lawyer, but she has barely enough money after rent and her monthly expenses. She has only begun to get her head above water. The university's pay is low, but that is expected at this early stage of her career. She had just developed wings, only to have them immediately clipped. Mini cannot believe her ill fortune. That night, she tosses and turns in her bed, invoking the Goddess and seeking her guidance. 'Help me, Ma Durga,' she cries in her sleep, 'save me from this wretched life.'

The next morning, although Mini has barely gotten any sleep, she arises refreshed—an acorn of an idea germinating in her mind. She thinks about it, marinating it in her mind through classes, then back at home. 'Yes,' she thinks, 'it is not a plan, but it will save my soul.'

A few weeks later, Alok returns. It is 9 p.m. when her doorbell rings and as Mini never has any visitors, she is certain it is him. She goes to the door, her heart in her mouth. She grips her mobile phone. She opens the door but keeps the latch on so he cannot enter.

She is right. Alok is standing in the dimly lit hallway. His hair is unkempt, his eyes are red and he looks wild. He smells of alcohol.

'What do you want?' she asks firmly.

'When will you sign the papers?' he demands.

'What papers?' she replies, as if she knows nothing of the lawyer's papers.

'You lying bitch!' he yells. 'Open the door and I'll show you—'

Before he can move, Mini slams the door shut. Alok proceeds to bang on the door with all his might.

'Leave now or I'm calling the police,' she shouts.

He continues to bang on the door.

Mini dials the Kolkata police number and puts the call on speakerphone. 'Here, you don't believe me. I've called the cops,' she calls out loudly.

A policeman answers the helpline and Mini starts to tell

him that there's a man at the door trying to get into her house. The banging stops. The policeman notes down her address and promises to send a police van shortly. In the hallway, Mini can hear steps receding. She breathes a sigh of relief.

Two police officers arrive at her flat an hour later. One of them is a woman. Mini files her complaint and they take down her statement. They also take down the statements of Mini's neighbours.

Weeks pass by uneventfully, but Mini is always on her guard. She looks over her shoulder when she walks home and always has the police officer's number on speed dial.

At work, her paintings take a different turn. She begins to paint scenes of domestic abuse, and they are wild and visceral. They are different from anything she has ever worked on—the colours are loud, the bodies twisted in horror and the women beautiful but tortured. She decides to make this series, which she entitles 'Hell on Earth', the focus of her next exhibition. Her canvases are larger than life and thus awe-inspiring to viewers. When her exhibition goes live, it becomes an instant sensation. The gallery extends the show for two whole months because there is always an endless throng of people coming to view it. Art critics and journalists sing her praises and the images go viral on social media.

But it is a certain woman, Vaishnavi, a women's rights activist, who is struck most by them. She cannot believe that these are works of fiction. She believes that the artist has endured everything the paintings convey. After all, art can only reflect life. Vaishnavi requests a meeting with Mini.

It is on a Sunday afternoon that the two women meet. Vaishnavi is twenty-five and has the invincibility of youth. She is relaxed when she sits opposite Mini in the teacher's common room at the university.

'I'll get straight to the point,' she says, lazily taking a sip of her coffee. 'Your works have blown my mind in a way nothing has in a long time. They are about your life, aren't they? Because I have never before come across the language of painting this way. I believe I have read this language correctly?'

Mini is shaken by the young lady's candour and composure. She assumed Vaishnavi was going to ask her the usual questions about her work: her influence, the challenges of being a self-taught artist, her goals, etc., so she feels obliged to be honest with her. 'Yes,' Mini replies.

'How bad was it?' Vaishnavi asks. She pauses, then says, 'Or shall I say…how *is* it? Because I can help you.'

Vaishnavi proceeds to tell Mini about her work as a women's activist, the stories of women she has helped, inspiring Mini with the possibilities for change.

Mini sighs. There is no point lying to this woman, she thinks. It serves her, Mini, no purpose. 'How much time do you have?' Mini asks with a smile.

'All the time in the world,' Vaishnavi replies.

Mini begins slowly—from the very beginning of her marriage to Alok, telling Vaishnavi about his mercurial temper, the nights he would come home drunk, the beatings, all unprovoked, how she ended up in hospital twice, how he'd broken her face, ribs and shins, how she had run away with nothing to call her own, no money, no belongings, how her parents had died shortly after her marriage and she had no one in the world to call her own since she had been an only child, how she had found her way to the slum, and then how her art had saved her.

Vaishnavi listens to Mini attentively. She looks older than her years. She takes notes, interrupting Mini only to ask a few questions. The hours pass.

When Mini finishes her story, Vaishnavi says, 'It's good you already filed a police complaint but now we must file a formal one for abuse and threat to your life. I will help you get it done.'

Before leaving, she turns to Mini and hugs her. 'I give you my word, Mini, you will be free from this hell soon enough.'

Nine months later, Mini is hurrying down Camac Street for her class, which is called 'The Language of Painting'. It is immensely popular, with 150 people enrolled for this session. Since she and Vaishnavi registered a case against Alok for domestic violence after their first meeting at the university, Mini's story has been published by the press many times, garnering the love and support of the public. Her artworks sell out almost immediately. She is invited to lectures and talks and is also an active member of women's organizations too. She has made enough money to make the down payment for a modest two-bedroom flat in central Kolkata. Finally, she will have a home she can truly call her own.

Mini runs across the busy street, narrowly missing a speeding taxi. The driver sticks his head out of the car window and hurls an abuse at her before whizzing away. Mini laughs. She knows it is her fault. But nothing—not even death itself—can bring her down.

She has just come from the family court where not only her divorce has been granted but Vaishnavi has called to tell her that her now ex-husband, Alok, has also been convicted by the district court, found guilty, and sentenced to fifteen years. She has never felt so free in her life. And this freedom courses through her veins like honey—pure and entirely her own.

8

Kintsugi

The bus has halted at a traffic light. Though only a few minutes have passed, the stop feels like eternity. Despite all the windows being open, there is not a whisper of breeze to ease the stifling atmosphere inside the vehicle. It is the peak of summer and this May afternoon bears down with unrelenting force.

Inside the bus, two children in matching school uniform pester their mother, who swats at the boy with a hint of irritation. 'Why can't you sit still for a minute?' she snaps. Across from them, a woman in a vibrant *dhakai* sari vigorously fans herself with a newspaper, seeking relief from the oppressive heat. Meanwhile, a young man leans his head outside the window, yearning for a breath of fresh air. The aisle is crammed with sweaty passengers, each eagerly anticipating their stop.

As the traffic light finally changes to green, the bus revs into motion, navigating the bustling roads of Park Street, skirting past Kolkata's most touristy area—the famous bookshops, lively cafes, acclaimed restaurants, and chic boutiques. Groups of foreigners stroll down the arched corridors, excitedly talking to each other. With backpacks slung casually over their shoulders, seemingly as light as candy floss, the heat does not seem to dampen the spirits of those enjoying their holiday.

Monica Chatterjee only takes the bus two days a week. On these occasions, the family car is otherwise occupied, and since her parents don't want her travelling alone in a taxi, the bus is her go-to option. On any other day, Monica cherishes the opportunity to observe the passing scenery, which is why she always grabs a window seat. Park Street is her favourite part of Kolkata. Typically, she finds herself lost in daydreams, imagining what it would be like to live in the charming old buildings adorned with Victorian flourishes and wooden staircases. What it would be like to throw open the grand windows and gaze down upon the busy streets below! However, today, the heat envelops her with its vice grip. Sweat beads trickle down her forehead and face, dampening her kurta, while even her scalp gleams with perspiration. If it hadn't been for the two classes at college, I would've bunked, she muses, though deep down she knows herself too well.

Monica loves her college. She never misses any classes. She is pursuing women's studies for her bachelor's degree and was top of the class in her first year. While most of her classmates seem to be doing the course as a fallback option, Monica lives and breathes it. She is inspired by her teachers and professors who simplify complex concepts and ideas of post-colonial theory and feminist theory as if they were children's stories. When Monica had first bought the books listed in the syllabus—she could hardly make sense of them—but with every class, the ideas glow brighter and firmly take root in her mind. The best part of her day is when she gets ready for college, looking forward to the mornings like a child awaiting their birthday.

The bus screeches to a halt at a stop. There is a frenzied push and shove at the doors as passengers jostle to disembark and newcomers scramble to find a footing to hop on simultaneously. Monica rummages through her backpack for her handkerchief, finally locating it and mops the sweat from her face. Never in her twenty years has she experienced a hotter summer day nor sweltering as this.

The bus driver's sharp honk signal his imminent departure from the stop. In the next moment, the bus jerks forward, prompting a slight breeze to slip through the open windows. Monica closes her eyes, relishing the respite from the relentless heat. When she reopens them, she looks around to notice fresh faces replacing the old ones. Some new passengers have gotten lucky to secure seats. Just as she is about to redirect her attention to the window, something catches her eye.

Up ahead, a few steps behind the bus driver's seat, she notices a face that strikes a chord of familiarity. The man stands tall, which is why she can see him past the other passengers crowding the aisle. Though wiry, his strong jaw remains clenched. His hair is patted down with oil to one side. He has long lashes that make his eyes seem darker than they are. Monica cannot help but stare. Sensing a gaze upon him, he turns to look around, his eyes scanning across the many people in the bus. She can now see his full face. Her heart starts pounding. *Could it be him?* Her mind screams with uncertainty. Just before the man's gaze meets hers, Monica lowers her head, pretending to look at her backpack that she has placed between her knees. He has not seen her, but she has, and the encounter sends her body and mind into a state of shock. A whirlwind of thoughts race through her mind in a mere second.

It cannot be…

But those eyes…

How can it be him?

How can you forget those eyes and that face…

But I had already found him…

Perhaps I had been wrong…

How could I be wrong?

After everything that happened…

'Are you ready or not?' Monica calls out to her younger sister, Dharna. 'It's about to start any minute now.'

'Coming, Didi, just one second!' Dharna's voice echoes from upstairs.

Monica can hear the frantic slam of their dressing table drawer, followed by the hurried thud of footsteps on the floorboards. Despite her irritation, she can't help but smile. Finally eighteen, Monica has earned her mother's permission to wear makeup for Durga Pujo, obviously on the condition that she keeps her grades up. Mrs Chatterjee, a strict authoritarian and successful lawyer, insists on maintaining a respectable image for her daughters. Every morning leading up to the festivities, she seizes any opportunity to lecture them on proper decorum.

'Yes, I know it is Durga Pujo and that everyone in Bengal seems to lose their minds during this time of the year, but that does not mean you both should follow suit. It is just a festival. Enjoy yourselves, seek Durga Ma's blessings, and be back home by 10 p.m. at the latest. Not a minute later. I don't want my daughters dressed up like mannequins for all the neighbourhood boys to ogle at. No talking to strangers, no wandering off too far, and certainly no flirting with boys. You will have plenty of time for all that once you've completed your education and secured good jobs. Do I make myself clear, ladies?' Mrs Chatterjee's words are a familiar refrain.

'Yes, Ma,' the two girls would drawl.

'I'm here,' Dharna says as she flies downstairs, breathless.

'Let's find a place to sit,' Monica suggests. 'The living room is already full.'

Sure enough, the room is filled to the brim. In the centre of the living room, the *thakur moshai* sits. Family members and relatives surround him, leaving little space. The sisters manage to find a spot at the back.

It's a long-standing tradition in the Chatterjee household

to have their family pundit recite the 'Mahishasura Mardini', a hymn from the 'Devi Mahatmya' on Mahalaya. This ritual marks an auspicious start to the day, believed to invoke the blessings of Goddess Durga. Many people rise before dawn to tune in to the special radio broadcast of this hymn, a tradition in India since the 1930s. Outside, it is still dark, but within the Chatterjee house, the atmosphere is lively with the chatter of relatives. As the thakur moshai prepares to begin, Monica's mother drapes her head with the pallu of her sari and requests everyone to keep silent. Before commencing his recitations, the thakur moshai offers the children present in the room a brief synopsis of why Durga Pujo is celebrated.

'According to legend,' thakur moshai begins, 'Mahishasura, the king with the head of a buffalo, was a devout worshipper of Lord Brahma. Pleased with Mahishasura's years of penance, Brahma offered him a boon. Mahishasura asked for immortality, wishing that he could not be killed by any 'man or animal' on Earth. Brahma granted his wish, but with a caveat—that a woman would end up killing him. Mahishasura scoffed at the idea. How could a woman cause him, the mighty king, any harm?'

'Intoxicated by the power of immortality, Mahishasura attacked the three realms of Earth, Heaven and Hell known as Trilok, and even tried to capture the kingdom of Lord Indra. The Gods became enraged with this upstart king and decided to wage war against him. However, they found themselves at an impasse due to Brahma's wish. Seeking a solution, they went to Lord Vishnu for aid. Lord Vishnu thought deeply about the situation and then finally devised a plan. He decided to create a female form that was strong enough to defeat Mahishasura.'

'But first, they approached Lord Shiva, the God of Destruction. After their congress, the three deities—Brahma, Vishnu and Shiva—combined their powers together and created Durga, the incarnation of Goddess Parvati, daughter of Himavan, lord of the mountains. Durga assumed the role of Mother Goddess, Shakti—the divine force that sustains the universe. And that is why we celebrate Ma Durga or Durga Pujo as you will call it in the coming days.'

'And now, I will begin the recitation.' The thakur moshai clears his throat. 'Mahalaya is a joyous occasion. On this day, Ma Durga begins her journey from Mount Kailash, where she resides with her husband Lord Shiva, to her maternal home on Earth. Beginning today, Ma Durga will undertake a week-long journey with her children—Ganesha, Kartik, Lakshmi and Saraswati—on a vehicle of her choice. I will begin with *Jago Tumi Jago.*'

Jago.... Tumi ja..go
Jago Durga Jago Dashaproharanodaarinee
Abhaya Shokti Baloprodayini Tumi Jago
Jago Tumi Ja...go.
Pronami Baroda Ajara Atula
Pronami Baroda Ajara Atula
Bahubaladhaarinee Ripudalabaarinee
Jago Maa, Sharanmayi, Chandika Shankari

Jago, Jago Maa, Jago Asurobinashinee
Tumi Jago...'

As the thakur moshai recites the numerous mantras, Monica finds it difficult to keep her eyes open. She has pins and needles in one leg and decides to get up and stretch. She quietly makes her way out of the room. Lucky we got a seat at the back, she reflects, glancing around to see if her mother has noticed her. However, her mother remains engrossed in the hymn, listening with an unwavering devotion.

Outside, on the verandah, Monica sits on the cane chair and massages her feet back to life from the numbness. The dawn air carries a refreshing chill, while the sweet scent of parijat flowers, falling at this hour, fills the atmosphere. The moon casts its gentle glow across the pale grey sky as the horizon blushes with the first rays of the sun. In the background, the thakur moshai's voice rumbles softly. Monica takes a deep breath. She can't remember the last time she had been awake at this hour. Given that this is her final school year, with aspirations to study medicine afterward, Monica finds herself always studying into the night. In fact, the only time she has seen dawn is when she is closing her books to crash heavily into sleep. So she decides to take a walk and savour this sacred morning, relishing this fleeting moment of freedom.

She walks down the crunchy gravel path and opens the gate. She slips out, wondering what her mother would think if she were to find her gone. The thought sends a rush of adrenaline through her, and with a giggle, she quickens her pace down the small path. The Chatterjee house is tucked away in the corner of the neighbourhood. The house next door was once a beautiful old Kolkata building which has been sold for a fortune to developers, who now plan to erect a six-story apartment complex in its place. Currently, only the skeleton of the new building stands, surrounded by piles of cement, iron rods and other construction materials. Monica wants to go to the neighbourhood park which has a small pond and beautiful old trees with benches beneath their shade. Previously, Monica would have to take the path all around the neighbourhood to get to the park, but now since the demolition of the old bungalow, she enjoys a shorter and more direct access to the park.

The gate is always kept open due to the daily comings and goings of the building company. Monica steps into the compound and makes her way past the piles of concrete slabs and cement with caution. She treads carefully, watchful of any stray nails that could pose a danger. She is halfway across the construction site when she hears something. She stops to scan her surroundings. There is no one nearby and the ground floor that is being built lies empty in darkness. She turns around to continue, but the hairs on her hand stand on end. Her heart beats faster, sensing the presence of something or someone beside her. She begins to panic, prompting her to increase her pace. However, before she can react further, a hand grabs her waist, while the other clamps down on her mouth.

Monica's eyes widen in fear. The man who holds her spins her around. He is much taller than her, with his oily hair slicked flat against his scalp. He has a strong jawline and deep-set dark eyes, with hollows around them. He wears a dirty white vest and a striped lungi. At first, she is in shock and when she finally tries to scream, he smacks her hard on her face and she falls on the ground. Her face stings with pain. Before she can do anything, the assailant pins her down, the full weight of his body bearing down on her petite frame. With brute force, he tears at her dress, his hand pressed down on her mouth.

Monica attempts to scream but no sound emerges from her throat. Frozen on the dirty ground, she feels utterly helpless as the assailant lifts her dress and violates her. He stinks of paan and body odour. She retches into her closed palm, but the man does not relent. He grunts above her for what feels like an eternity, until finally, he departs, leaving her shattered and alone.

She lies there on the ground, amidst the debris of the unfinished building that once stood as their neighbour's warm home. It was a place where she and her sister frolicked with the other children, playing catch and climbing the mango tree in the summer. It was always open and safe for them to roam about freely at any time of the day.

She cranes her neck, squinting into the distance. There, faintly visible, she thinks she can see the lights of the Chatterjee house, her lovely home. It's where the thakur moshai chants the hymns of the great Ma Durga, depicting her descent to

Earth to kill the beast Mahishasura with her mighty trident.

Monica feels as though she has no option but to tell her parents everything.

She longs to retreat to her room and hide forever. She wishes the earth would open up, as it once did for Sita, and she could disappear into its depths.

However, when she returns home, she finds everyone gathered there. The recitations have concluded, the thakur moshai is wrapping up, and Mrs Chatterjee is greeting all her guests goodbye. As Monica steps onto the veranda, Mrs Chatterjee catches sight of her daughter. Monica is dishevelled, her dress is torn, and there's a cut on her cheek that is bleeding.

Mrs Chatterjee shrieks. She rushes to Monica and guides her to her bedroom. There, Monica falls into her arms and tells her everything. Tears stream down their faces as her mother whispers softly, 'I'm sorry, my poor child,' into the daughter's ear.

Once the relatives have departed, Monica's mother emerges, her eyes red from crying. She pulls her husband aside and talks to him. Mr Chatterjee is unable to sit upon hearing the news. He paces the floor of his study anxiously. 'We will have justice,' he finally declares after a moment of contemplation.

'After all, you are a respected lawyer and I am a retired civil servant, for God's sake. If this can happen to our daughter, then it is lawlessness out there. I will not stand for it, goddammit,' he yells.

Mr Chatterjee immediately contacts the commissioner of police, a close friend of his, and briefs him on the incident. They are advised to take Monica to the hospital immediately for a medical examination and DNA preservation, followed by a visit to Dum Dum police station to file a report.

'If there is one thing I can guarantee you, Mr Chatterjee, it's that I will find the rogue responsible for this and ensure they rot in prison,' the commissioner assures Mr Chatterjee.

Following that fateful morning of Mahalaya, the ensuing days are a blur for Monica. She complies with every request made of her. After all, she thinks to herself, it was not listening to her mother that led to her plight. Thus, she undergoes medical tests, accompanies her parents to the police station to file a report, and dutifully answers all the questions the officers ask her. Though they are patient and gentle, she finds these interrogations intrusive and repulsive. She does not want to remember the memories, yet she is reminded that justice hinges on her ability to recall the events.

Through it all, Monica remains focussed on her studies for her finals. It is the only thing she wants to do. However, she doesn't want to pursue medicine anymore. Instead, she discovers a newfound passion for a course at Calcutta University—gender and women studies. She believes she must study this and later pursue endeavours that will positively impact the lives of women.

Dharna tries to talk to her sister but all she encounters

is a closed door. Her elder sister has changed and something within her has died.

A week later, Monica finds herself back at the police station where she is ushered into a room with a glass window. Peering through the glass, she observes a lineup of men, all potential suspects. The police commissioner inquires whether she recognizes any of the individuals.

Monica feels sweat bead on her brow as her gaze shifts from one man to another, five in total. Immediately, she eliminates three of them from suspicion. She scrutinizes the remaining two, taking a long time, as she assesses each of them. In her mind, she is certain that one of them is not the culprit—he is not that tall or wiry. However, she is not a hundred percent sure that the final man is the one.

'Do you recognize the man?' The police commissioner asks her gently. 'You can take all the time you want... Please do not feel pressured.'

But Monica feels fuzzy and wants this ordeal to be over. She wants the man to be put behind bars, where he can never do what he did to her to any other woman ever. She makes up her mind and informs the police commissioner, 'It is him.'

'Are you completely sure?' he asks her.

'Yes,' Monica says. 'Can I go now?'

The police commissioner looks at her parents and then at Monica. 'Yes, child, you can go.'

A few months later, the case is taken to court, where the public defence attorney's argument is torn to shreds by the more qualified and adept private prosecutor hired by the

Chatterjees. After both sides present their cases, the judge declares the man guilty, handing down a sentence of life imprisonment.

As the proceedings conclude, Monica fixes a gaze on the guilty man. He sits, his face buried in his hands while two police officers escort him away. Her parents embrace her tightly before guiding her to their car.

Despite the closure of the trial, Monica feels a heavy numbness within her.

✍

Monica realizes she is two stops past her destination.

Once the tumultuous thoughts in her mind quieten, she regains her focus. Now she is certain that the man behind the driver's seat, the one preparing to disembark, is the perpetrator—the beast who assaulted her three years ago on that fateful morning of Mahalaya. She has not been this certain of anything before in her life.

Thoughts of the man she identified in the line-up, now languishing in jail, flood her mind. Her blood boils with anger—for the horrors inflicted upon her, for the suffering she endured, and for what another was undergoing.

Monica isn't certain of her plan, but she's determined to follow the real criminal and find out where he lives. Even if it means waiting on this bus indefinitely, she is ready to do it.

At the next stop, the man gets off, and Monica follows suit, slipping out through the back exit. Monica keeps her distance as the man begins to make his way through the crowded by-lanes. Monica discreetly captures a few photographs of him, his towering height making him hard to miss, until he leads her to a decrepit building.

She watches as he ascends the steps and disappears into the building. Stopping at the building's entrance, Monica hesitates to follow him inside. Instead, she notices a hardware shop on the ground floor, where a man stands at the counter, counting out bolts.

Monica approaches the man at the counter. 'Excuse me,' she speaks calmly, 'the man that just went up the steps... Does he live here?'

'Who?' The man barely looks at her.

'The tall man... I was speaking to him about a construction job but forgot to get a few details from him,' she says confidently.

'Binoy? Yes, he does. Top floor. Watch your step,' the man replies briskly, returning to this counting.

Monica's heart is racing. 'Thank you,' she says, quickly turning around and hastening out of the neighbourhood.

Back at home, just before dinner time, Monica gathers her parents and insists on speaking with them. Mr Chatterjee leads them to his office and the three of them sit down.

Monica tells them about what she saw on the bus and what she did after. She asks them what she needs to do, unable to live with a guilty conscience. She has sent an innocent man to prison while the real criminal evades justice. Who knows how many more women he has assaulted and how many more will become his victims in the future.

The Chatterjees' are shocked by the news.

'Are you absolutely sure, Mon?' her mother inquires.

'Yes, Ma. I've never been more certain of anything else in my life,' she asserts. 'You have to believe me.'

Mrs Chatterjee turns to her husband, who remains silent. He stares at his feet while his fingers are tightly clasped on his lap.

'Leave the room,' he commands without looking up.

Monica gets up to leave, but as she reaches the door, she turns to address her father, 'Baba, if you could save another eighteen-year-old from enduring the revolting ordeal I went through, wouldn't you?'

A penetrating silence engulfs the room.

'What should we do?' Mrs Chatterjee asks.

'It is clear, isn't it?' her husband responds.

'To go through that hell all over again? I don't know if I can do it…'

'This is not about you…'

'But just think about—'

'Think about what?' Mr Chatterjee snaps. 'Just think about that morning when Mon arrived in that state. Just think about Dharna, our daughter, who is unsafe every day going to school. Just think about all those girls… all of them innocent… and any minute that innocence could be snatched away from them by brutes. *Brutes*!'

Mrs Chatterjee remains silent.

Mr Chatterjee stands up and speaks in a menacing tone.

'I will put the criminal in the place he belongs if that's the last thing I do in this life.'

After consulting with the police commissioner, Mr Chatterjee learns that his daughter's case can be reopened on the grounds of wrongful conviction.

'But it's not that simple...' the commissioner says on the phone. 'If you want to appeal the judge's decision and reopen the case, you need good justification. To reopen the case, you must take the following actions. Submit an appeal to the court demonstrating the flaws in the judgment. You must convincingly demonstrate the mistakes in the conclusion because it is a highly technical and complex process. After that, your attorney must analyse the trial transcript and craft a brief mentioning the errors that could impact the outcome. This brief will be filed in an upper court, and the opposing counsel will respond. The appellant court will then hear the oral argument following this. The panel will analyse all the evidence and facts, and issue a written decision.

'You will then need to speak to the district attorney regarding the matter, issue a warrant for the real criminal's arrest, and collect DNA evidence from the man. They would then need to match the DNA samples to the ones preserved from Monica's tests—assuming they have not been destroyed.'

After exhausting all their leads, it becomes clear that

they will not achieve the justice they strive for. Monica is devastated by this. She spends her days in a blur of research and conversations with lawyers, but all of it lead to the same conclusion: an innocent man languishes in jail while the real criminal remains free.

Six months after applying for a visit, Monica finally stands at the visitor's section of Dum Dum Central Correction Home. She signed countless papers and forms to be here, and even today, she has had to sign a few more. She has also been briefed on the dos and don'ts for visitors. The prison conditions are appalling. The system of prison visitors is still considered by prison staff as an unnecessary intrusion in their work, and non-official visitors reduce their functions to mere clerical formality in the absence of any accountability.

A prison warden announces a name. 'Bharat Bhushan.'

Monica's ears prick up. She stands straight, observing as the warden brings in a bearded man who walks with a severe hunch.

The man's cheeks are gaunt and the hollows under his eyes are deep as still pools. His hands and feet are cuffed with heavy iron. He looks nothing like Monica remembers. He has aged ten years in the past four.

The warden points to a table with two chairs and roughly shoves Bharat towards one.

'No need to push,' Bharat snaps angrily at the warden.

The warden scoffs and goes to stand at one end of the room.

This is the visiting hour at the prison, and similar scenes play out across the room. There is a mix of conversation and crying, shouting and sobbing, and occasionally, there's even laughter.

'You…' Bharat says to Monica. 'You got me here, now what do you want from me?'

Monica is frozen. She cannot bring herself to even sit down.

'Do you know what happens to "rapists" in prison?'

When she doesn't speak, Bharat spits the words from gritted teeth, 'No, of course you won't. I had a child, a daughter, and a wife. All of whom are now begging on the streets because I, the only bread earner, am here. But what can I say to you, madam?'

Finally, the words burst out of Monica's throat. 'I-I've come here to apologize. I'm sorry. I know you are innocent. I know this because as fate would have it, I came across the real criminal some time ago. I have been trying very hard to get you out but…'

Here she stops. She does not have the courage to tell this man, this stranger, that she has failed him once again.

Bharat watches her intently. Then, he looks at the table and bursts out laughing. 'You know I am innocent now! That is a great joke, young lady. You should be a clown at a circus.'

'I'm really sorry,' she sits down. 'I will do anything to help you and your family. Just tell me what I should do?'

Bharat looks her in the eye, and after a moment, he says, 'You can do this… Go find my family and help them. They need all the help they can get. And stay the hell away from me.' He rises forcefully from his chair. 'Warden,' he yells. 'Take me back, now!'

Monica watches Bharat leave the room with the prison warden. He does not look back. He doesn't waste a minute. It is almost as if he can't get away from her quickly enough.

On her way out, Monica bursts into tears.

That night, Monica is unable to sleep. She tosses and turns on her bed, the image of Bharat in chains haunting her thoughts.

She consoles herself, reasoning that she was just a child at the time. The pressure of the police system to pick someone out of a lineup was immense, and the psychological urgency of making a decision in those circumstances was even greater. She was just human and humans make mistakes. Big mistakes.

But no matter how much she reassures herself, she cannot shake away the look on Bharat's face. He was a broken man, devastated by a child's decision, shattered by the judiciary, the prison system and the separation from his family.

Monica tosses the covers aside and gets up. She throws open the bedroom window and fresh air wafts in. How many Bharats must be in these prisons, she thinks, facing a lifetime of wrongful conviction? How many innocent men die behind bars while real criminals remain free? Why isn't anyone doing anything about it?

Outside, dawn is breaking and the pale sunlight dilutes the inky night sky.

Monica cannot let this go. Just as the sun creeps over the earth, she knows what she must do. She will change her course, study law, and start an organization for those who are wrongfully convicted. It means sacrificing two years of her education to begin afresh, but she knows she can do it.

If not for Bharat, she will fight for others. So that one day, they too can step out from the shadows of the night into mornings like this—cool and crisp—and watch the sunrise as free humans do.

Seven years have passed. Monica now runs a non-profit organization where she works tirelessly to exonerate men and women, bringing them into her rehabilitation centre and helping them rebuild their shattered lives for a new start. Every day, she strategizes ways to secure Bharat's freedom.

www.ingramcontent.com/pod-product-compliance
Lightning Source LLC
Chambersburg PA
CBHW031959010726
47493CB00007B/2258